A Gift from a Goddess
A Legend To Love

Maggi Andersen

A Gift from a Goddess
A Legend to Love (Book 9)
Copyright © 2018 by Maggi Andersen

Cover by Midnight Muse Designs:
http://midnightmusedesigns.com

Edited by D. Coleman
BK Editing Services

ISBN 13: 978-0-6482931-2-5

Join Maggi's Newsletter for sales, free books, and to learn about new releases.
http://eepurl.com/cEqK9b

Prologue

Greece, 1819.

"AH, GREECE." LEWIS, Lord Chesterton, took a deep breath of pine-scented air, glad to have left behind the cheerlessness and chill of London. He followed his friend, Damen Savakis out of the shady forest into the sunshine. They pushed their way through dense patches of gorse and brier and climbed the steep rocky hill toward the ruined temple.

He had first met Damen a few summers ago when he'd rescued Lewis from heat exhaustion. He'd been wandering around the Acropolis in Athens and lost track of the time. A poet, Damen had studied at Oxford, but preferred the warmth of the Greek climate and the simple life.

As they struggled up the steep incline, they left behind the grove of silver olive trees and black cypresses, and the dusky red roofs of the village where Damen lived with his wife and unruly children. Above them, the Temple of Aphrodite stood silent, outlined against an azure sky.

On reaching the temple, Lewis ran his hands over one of the remaining six sun-warmed marble pillars left standing, and imagined he breathed in the same air as the ancients.

"It's good to be here," he said turning to his friend.

"Naturally, I am pleased to see you," Damen said as he perched on a stone slab. "But surprised you've come now. Your latest work has just been lauded, has it not? Would you not wish to remain and enjoy the accolades?"

Lewis shrugged. The *ton* was fickle in its praise. They preferred to spread vicious lies about him. He was tired after toiling over his last commission for the Duke and Duchess of Rollins. One of his low moods threatened. The sculpture now stood in their great hall. He'd wanted the statue of Diana the Huntress to be perfect, and she very nearly was.

Damen's dark eyes studied him. "Might the reason you're here be a lady?"

"Indirectly." Lewis couldn't blame his periods of despair on Adela. He just had to grit his teeth and wait for the mood to lift. And how much easier it was here rather than London where gray skies and low moods went hand in hand.

"Your mistress?" Damen persisted.

His friend wanted to help. But Lewis wished he wouldn't. "Adela accused me of cheating with one of my models."

"Not your style is it?"

Lewis swept back his dark hair and grimaced. "No, but the model was a flirt. Women are not to be trusted, Damen."

Damen widened his eyes. "What happened?"

"While I was adjusting Marigold's pose, she kissed me. Unfortunately, Adela walked in at that precise moment. Naturally, she was cross."

Damen nodded, a smile lurking at the corners of his mouth. "Most unfortunate."

"A naked woman in my studio for hours makes me vulnerable to scandal, so I've become very cautious. I don't sleep with my models. But I accept that Adela was justified in being angry." Lewis glared at his friend who was not taking the matter seriously enough. "Adela stormed out, and I told my model, Marigold, that I no longer required her services. I then had another angry, weeping woman to deal with."

"And one with a perfect figure, eh?" Damen shook his head in commiseration. "A terrible position to be in, my friend."

Lewis frowned. "When I work, Damen, I think of little else. Adela found sculpting unsuitable for a lord of the realm. She considered a gentlemen's role was to squire their ladies about to balls and such during the Season."

"She wished for marriage?"

"Not Adela. Married at seventeen to an old man who made her life miserable, she enjoys her widowhood. She wasted no time in informing me about her new lover."

"You did not think of marriage?"

Lewis turned his attention to the rest of the elegant Doric columns, still remarkably intact. "A man and woman's relationship is one of mutual need, which can be satisfied outside marriage. I'm not in a hurry to fall into the parson's mouse trap again."

"You English call marriage a trap?" Damen shook his head. "A sorry way to view life, my friend."

It wasn't surprising Damen didn't agree. He and Evania enjoyed a tumultuous, passionate relationship which had produced a large brood of children. Whereas, Lewis and Laura, who were passionately in love when they first married, became mistrustful of each other. Then horror followed horror. Laura's violent death, and his sister, Emmaline's miscarriage.

"You Greeks are a nation of dreamers." Lewis waved his arm to encompass the ruined temple. "Just look around you. Mythology governs your lives. In my experience, women are mortal beings, not goddesses. And let's face it, we men are not gods." Lewis pushed away from the column. "Let's go down. I fancy some luncheon. I'd hoped to find inspiration for my next sculpture on this trip, but that hasn't happened."

Damen joined him as they slowly descended the steep hill. "Inspiration? I shall take you to see Aphrodite's Rock at Papos in Cyprus."

"Cyprus? That's a long way."

"Ah, but it is known as the birthplace of Aphrodite," Damen said as they picked their way over rocks scattering loose dirt. "We'll sail there in my uncle's fishing boat. It should take no more than a month or two."

Lewis frowned. "I planned to return to London to begin work before the heat of summer makes the studio insufferable. Are you sure the journey will be worth it?"

"In Kouklia there's a fragment of mosaic that you must see."

They reached level ground and made their way along the dirt road toward Damen's house.

"According to the legend, Gaia, the Mother Earth, asked one of her sons, Cronus, to mutilate his father, Uranus, the Greek god of the sky," Damen said. "Cronus cut off Uranus' male parts and threw them into the sea from which, born of the sea foam, Aphrodite arose from the waves."

Lewis grunted. "I planned to see some ancient statuary, Damen." But he thought of the beautiful work by the artist, Sandro Botticelli, *The Birth of Venus*, the Roman's name for Aphrodite, painted in the 15th century which he'd viewed in Florence. The beautiful goddess blown to shore on a scallop shell by the wind god, Zephyr. "Although, you have me intrigued."

"Good. Come. You will be glad you did."

At Papos a month later, after viewing the extraordinary rock formation where the sea swirled and tossed up a column of sea foam, said to form into a woman's body, they moved on to the ancient town of Kouklia where the ruins of a larger and more impressive temple of Aphrodite awaited them.

Lewis surveyed the remnants of the splendid mosaic of Leda and the Swan. "That's the most exquisite bottom I've ever seen." He turned to Damen. "Thank you. You have given me my inspiration."

Damen laughed. "You do her great disservice. Aphrodite is a powerful goddess. She stands for love, beauty, pleasure and procreation." He studied Lewis, his smile slipping away. "She can even mend a broken heart."

"She can do all that?" Lewis shook his head and smiled mirthlessly. "Hogwash. But wouldn't it be nice if it were true."

Chapter One

London, 1819

"IF YOU COULD just move your leg a little to the right..." Alberto Bertoletti stroked a hand up Hebe's leg.

She slapped it away as his fingers crept higher. "Just tell me what you want, Alberto. I can move without your help."

The Italian painter sighed. "You are the most frustrating model I have ever used." He threw up his hands and turned to the painting on the easel. "Look at this work. It is lifeless! Can't you unbend a little? Artists need more from their models. A little affection. How can I paint a passionate work? You are meant to be my muse."

Hebe rose from the pile of cushions and wrapped the sheet carefully around herself.

"Now what are you doing?" Alberto roared. "I've hardly painted a stroke today."

"Because you've been more intent on seducing me." Hebe glared at him. "If I wanted to be a courtesan, I would be one."

"If you weren't such a good model, I would have thrown you out days ago," he said sulkily.

She rubbed her arms. A cold draft always wafted into the loft from somewhere. It was a wonder she hadn't gotten sick. She picked up her clothes and began to dress. "Then I shall save you the trouble. And I'd like to be paid for the work I've done, please."

"I don't see why I should..."

"Unless you want me to tell all the models that you don't pay?"

When Hebe arrived home an hour later at their small townhouse in Cheapside, her mother met her at the door. "Why are you home so early?"

"The innkeeper let me go early today." Hebe opened her reticule and took out the coins. "Here's the money for the week."

Her mother took it. "My poor girl, working as a maid! I trust you came home in a hackney. I hate to think of you traveling about unescorted." She sighed. "To think it has come to this. Your father would never have wanted..."

Hebe no longer listened. She climbed the stairs to her room.

"Have you given more thought to marrying Mr. Wainscott?" Her mother asked, following her up the stairs. "I know he's far beneath us socially but seems a decent man and has not changed his mind. He called this morning to inquire after you."

The expression in Mr. Wainscott's eyes, when she'd last seen him, was a curious mix of pity and longing. Hand on the banister, Hebe swung around. "I think I'd rather die than marry him, Mama."

"Oh. Yes. I understand, Hebe." Her mother raised her reddened hands to Hebe's face. "A pity he isn't more attractive. He would take care of us and you wouldn't have to do such dreadful work."

Hebe averted her eyes from her mother's reddened skin. The sight of it tore at her heart. Mama had once been proud of her beautiful hands.

Her mother retreated, and Hebe shut the door to her room. She took out the box she kept in the bottom of her wardrobe and dropped in the few coins she'd held back. Then she sat before the mirror. She removed the pins from her hair and brushed her long fair locks. The shock of the last year had begun to ebb leaving a hollowness in her chest. She was determined to rise above the scandal that had enveloped her and her mother when her beloved father died. It had left Hebe's Season in ruins, while her suitors faded away. Gentlemen began to make discreet offers for her to become their mistress, and men who would never have approached her before, stepped forward prepared to rescue her from her fate; men who were too old, or like Mr. Wainscott, a widower left with children to raise.

She stared at her wan face in the mirror. With the family's country house and their townhouse in Mayfair, both sold, they'd moved into this depressing narrow little house with just a maid and a cook. The carriages and horses gone, and their staff, some of whom she had known all her life, all put off.

Hebe became determined to find a way to ease her mother's worries, but her attempts fell at the first hurdle. She was told she could never be a governess, she was too attractive, and the big houses demanded staff with some experience.

While Hebe wandered the East End, she was befriended by Sally Green, who modelled regularly for a painter. Sally suggested Hebe try it and helped her find her first job.

So far, posing for artists kept her and her mother's heads above water, and allowed her to put a little away. Successful artists paid regularly and not all were like Alberto intent on seducing her.

Poor Father hadn't meant to leave them destitute. But he'd considered himself a failure after he'd become involved in some dubious financial scheme and lost most of his fortune. She and her mother only learned of it from the gossip mongers and broadsheets. He died leaving them in debt and burdened with the shame of suicide. Even his family had disowned them, and there was no one left from her mother's family. Apart from her father's sister in Brighton who showed no inclination to help them, they were entirely alone.

Hebe sighed and rose to change her gown. She refused to place her future in the hands of any man and was determined to make her own way in the world. And when there was enough money saved, she would.

Hebe spent the next afternoon roaming the artists' quarter. She shared a cup of tea with Sally while she took a break from posing in her artist lover's dreary attic. Sally pulled across the tatty curtain to hide the painter working at a canvas. The air was thick with the smells of oil paint and turpentine. Hebe wished they could open a window, but Sally was barely dressed, the thin robe stretched tight over ample curves.

"There's a gentleman looking for a new model." Sally tossed back her long red hair and blew into the cup she held with both hands. "He's very choosy, he's already rejected Dora and Liza."

They were both good models. Perhaps Hebe wouldn't be suitable either. "Who is he?"

"Viscount Chesterton. He has a studio in Mayfair."

"A wealthy man?"

"Yes. A sculptor," Sally said. "His work is very well considered."

"Marigold was modelling for some lord."

"She was. Him. But he let her go."

"Why? Didn't he treat her well?"

"He was horrid. She said he made her cry."

"Well, I'm not sure that I..."

"He gave her fifty pounds when he let her go."

Hebe stared. "Fifty pounds? What did she have to do for it?"

"Nothing, she said."

"I find that difficult to believe." Hebe frowned. "Perhaps he scared her into silence."

"Lawks!" Sally scoffed. "Marigold? I doubt a herd of bulls on the rampage through Pall Mall would scare her."

"Can't hurt to go and see him," Hebe said. "I am hardened to rudeness. But first I must speak to Marigold."

"She's posing for an artist in Holland Park."

"Who?"

"She didn't tell me. Marigold likes to keep secrets, doesn't trust us not to snatch the job from under her nose." Sally grinned. "Don't know why."

Two days later, in Mayfair, Hebe waited outside Lord Chesterton's residence, a handsome four-story townhouse in Mount Street. The butler who opened the door looked down his long nose at her. Hebe quickly explained about the note she'd sent and why she wished to see the sculptor.

"Please use the servants' entrance in future." He led the way past elegantly furnished rooms. At the rear of the house she went through a door that gave access to the narrow wooden servants' stairs, leading from the kitchens up to the attics. "You'll find his lordship in his studio at the top."

Hebe climbed the stairs, her breath shortening with nerves. Should she be here? Was the man a rake or a brute? She'd met lords who were known to be both during her short Season. She'd managed thus far to avoid baring all of herself, but she was prepared for the possibility, should he request it. Silly to be prudish about it. It was only a body after all. Still, some concerns niggled at her. Most artists were as poor as she was and consumed with their work. They were anxious to earn enough from their paintings to buy paints and canvases and pay their rent. This sculptor obviously didn't have those concerns. Why did he make Marigold cry? She wished she'd been able to find out. And why had he given her fifty pounds?

She came to the door at the very top and knocked.

"Come."

She opened the door and entered a large airy space where the sun shone through a glass ceiling. A gentleman stood, chisel and hammer in hand beside a large block of pale marble. He turned to her as she entered. "Yes?"

She stopped at the door, distracted by his penetrating gaze. Tall and dark-haired, he looked strong, and lean, and he frowned at her. Might he already have engaged a model? She half expected him to send her packing.

"I heard you was lookin' for a model, milord," she said, adopting Sally's manner of speech. "That's if you haven't found one."

"You heard correctly." He put the implements down on a table beside him, laden with different sized hammers, chisels, and files, then turned to study her.

Rendered nervous by his deep brown eyes she looked around. The studio was different to the painters' studios she'd worked in. Far larger, it was also clean, the air tinged with the lingering odor of coffee, and something delicious. Her empty stomach gurgled, disconcerting her further. The sun's rays brightened an exquisitely painted Italian screen standing in one corner and the crimson chaise longue placed before the block of marble. A table was piled high with books, journals, and boxes of pencils beside which was a Chippendale splat-back chair, like those they used to have at home.

And not a cold draft to be found.

"Well don't just stand there. Come in so I can see you." Lewis beckoned with an impatient hand. "Take off your hat and coat."

The young woman advanced cautiously into the room. He was caught by her quiet manner, more used to being greeted with a smart quip by hip swinging confident girls. She removed her straw bonnet drawing his eye to her abundant blonde hair, piled on her head as if she hadn't come to grips with how to contain it. She slipped her arms out of the garment of some indecipherable color. Beneath it, she wore a faded blue dress with short sleeves which exposed slender, nicely shaped arms. A ribbon of a darker blue was caught beneath breasts that promised to be shapely. When his artist's eye finished judging her proportions, he met her cornflower blue gaze which seemed to study him as critically as he did her.

A perfect artist's model she should be in great demand. Lewis walked over to her.

Her eyes widened, and she took a step back. "Will I suit?" she began, clutching her reticule, coat, and hat in her hands.

Was she new at this? "I shall have to see you as nature intended, of course, but I have great hopes that you will be perfect for my Aphrodite."

"Aphrodite?" she repeated, her eyes growing wide.

Well, it wouldn't matter if she wasn't too bright, he thought, although he found himself disappointed at the prospect. Might be asking too much. "An ancient Greek goddess," he explained. "Go behind that screen and undress. Slip on the robe you'll find hanging there. I shall need time to work out the best pose for the statue. It's my practice to make several drawings before I begin."

He watched her disappear behind the painted screen. "You've done this sort of work before?"

"Oh yes," she said, her voice muffled as if she had her dress over her head. "Never for a sculptor though. Painters."

"Why don't you continue to work for artists?"

Silence. "It was the smell."

"They smelled?"

A slight sound which could be a chuckle. "The paint and linseed oil made me sick."

"Nothing like that here." Lewis sorted through his charcoals. He was so eager to begin, he hadn't even asked her name.

Such concerns fled when she emerged. The robe better displayed her excellent figure and long slim legs. But what struck him most was her hair. Soft fair waves flowed to her waist lit with strands of gold. Delicate of feature, she moved with grace. Despite the way she spoke, she was nothing like his usual models.

"Your name?" he asked, almost as an afterthought.

"Hebe, milord."

"Hebe...?"

She hesitated. "Fenchurch."

She seemed reluctant to supply it. And she stared at him as if he might have heard of it. Oddly, Fenchurch did ring a distant bell somewhere in his brain. "Hebe? Well I'll be darned. That's an ancient Greek name. Is there a story behind it?"

"Me pa liked it." She firmed her lips as if refusing to explain further.

"Hebe was the goddess of youth." He made a swiveling motion with his finger. "Turn around for me." The name suited her. As she turned, he tapped his chin, searching for the right pose. Aware of her subtle perfume, he took in the graceful dip of her waist and the saucy jut of her bottom. "How did your father come across it?"

"It was in one of those publications. At the library. 'E was fond of the library."

"Was?"

Golden lashes hid her eyes. "Yes. 'E's gone now."

"I'm sorry." Lewis began to arrange her pose. He felt strangely out of sorts as if he'd dreamed her up. But her skin beneath his fingers as he moved her arm was real, smooth, and pale as a pearl.

"Sit down, Hebe." He backed away and walked over to ring the bell. "We'll have coffee before we begin."

"I'd be ever so grateful for a cup. Thank you, milord."

"Call me, Lewis, please. Society never ventures into this room unless invited." He went to the table to select his materials discovering a surprising eagerness to begin.

Chapter Two

AFTER TYING THE strings of her bonnet, Hebe descended the stairs leading to the kitchens. As the butler had requested, she left the house through the tradesmen's entrance.

Lord Chesterton, or rather, Lewis as he'd insisted she call him, was somewhat brusque in his manner, and did not seem in any way lustful, but it was too early to tell. She eased her shoulders as she made her way along the mews behind the house and into Carlos Street. She'd worked for several hours, adopting different poses, never once having to remove the robe. Strangely, it made her more self-conscious sitting there covered while he sketched in his book. How very odd. If it went on too long, it might be difficult to disrobe before him. To look on the bright side, she'd enjoyed a tasty lunch of chicken pie still warm from the oven, washed down with ale, and during the afternoon, they'd stopped again for coffee and iced cakes. None of her artists had ever fed her. And Lewis had asked her to come again tomorrow.

Despite discovering she had left a glove behind, she was quite perky as she reached the main thoroughfare and set off in search of a hackney. It was a long way to Cheapside. The cost would cut into her wages. But if the work was regular, she might manage to save a little.

Hebe yawned. She found remaining still in a pose surprisingly enervating. But she didn't mind how difficult or tiring it was if it brought her dream closer to reality. She was passionate about the future she held dear; a country cottage in a quiet village where her mother could rest and be peaceful, and Hebe could grow flowers for Covent Garden.

A hackney appeared at the end of the street, and she rushed forward and hailed it. She arrived home eager to remove her shoes, which pinched, only to find her mother entertaining Mr. Wainscott in the parlor. He jumped to his feet as she entered, his face adopting that look of quiet desperation.

When her mother left to organize the tea, Hebe had no choice but to entertain him.

He advanced on her, smelling oddly of camphor mixed with bay rum and making her shrink back in her seat.

"I have my heart set on you, Miss Fenchurch," he declared passionately, falling to his knee.

"Please do get up, sir!" Hebe said, horrified.

His plain face was suffused with color, his eyes wild. "I cannot go on without you!"

Someone knocked at the front door. "Please excuse me, Mr. Wainscott." Hebe jumped up and edged past him. "I must answer the door. It's the maid's day off."

She threw open the door ready to invite anyone who stood there inside. Her mouth dropped open. She never expected to find Lord Chesterton standing there dressed in a fine gray wool greatcoat. He swept off his hat and held her glove out to her as if it was of immense value. The one with the darned finger.

"You left this behind," he said with a smile. "As the weather is cool, you might have need of it." On the road outside stood an elegant landau with a groom at the heads of a pair of thoroughbred chestnuts.

She swallowed, and fairly snatched it from him, praying her mother wouldn't come to the door. "How did you know where to find me," she blurted.

"It was in your note."

What was she thinking? "How kind of you, sir," she murmured. "But you shouldn't have. Really." It would be frightfully rude not to invite him inside. "Er, would you care to....?"

"Who is it, Hebe?" her mother called from the kitchen stairs. "Why is that maid always occupied elsewhere when someone knocks at the door? Not the knife sharpener again is it?"

"No, Mama. A gentleman has kindly returned my glove," Hebe called desperately.

"Oh, very well then. But in future send Kitty."

Hebe's chest tightened as her mother's footsteps sounded on the stairs.

The viscount's black eyebrows rose. Intelligent brown eyes met hers, with a glimmer of understanding. "I must go," he said. "The horses dislike being kept standing."

"Oh, but, yes. Of course. In the cold breeze," she said gushing with relief. "And thank you again." She had to stop herself from dropping into a curtsey.

Hebe watched him stride across the road. By the time he'd regained his vehicle, her mother had joined her, but thankfully, was too well-mannered to peer out.

"I dropped my glove when I left the carriage," Hebe explained shutting the door with a snap. "A kind gentleman was passing."

Her mother peered at her. "You look quite flushed, Hebe."

"Yes. A headache coming on, I'm afraid."

"My dear, have you? I do hope you're not suffering from some malaise." Her mother cast an anxious glance at the parlor door. "And Mr. Wainscott is still waiting for his tea. I do wish you would make your feelings plain to him. He is still holding out hope."

Hebe put a hand to her forehead. She clamped her lips on the suggestion of giving him last week's stale cake in the hope he wouldn't call again. "Please make my excuses, Mama. I must lie down."

"Yes, of course, my dear. I'll be up as soon as I can with a tisane."

Hebe hadn't fibbed exactly, for her temples did throb, and it worsened every time she thought of Lewis' shrewd brown eyes. They seemed to take in a lot. Going over it again, she bit her lip. She was sure he would suspect she was not what she led him to believe. She disliked misleading him, but to confess the truth would mean he'd let her go. That must not happen. It was more than the money so desperately needed, she liked working with Lewis in such civilized surroundings. She saw no option but to continue the ruse until he spoke of it. Funnily enough, she rather liked the Hebe she'd become when she sat for him. The disguise was like a cloak she had donned, and while she was there in that beautiful studio the world outside ceased to matter.

"It was her voice." Lewis donned his hat as the carriage took him back to Mayfair to visit his sister.

The groom briefly took his gaze from the road. "Pardon, milord?"

"I'm talking to myself, John. Pay no heed."

Yes. Lewis affirmed. Her voice was different. As surprised as he was to find Miss Hebe Fenchurch living in reasonably comfortable lodgings, he accepted her need to work. But gone was the patois of the East End. Her refined speech belonged to the upper classes. Unmistakable. And her mother, who had called from the shadowy interior. There was a mystery here.

The discovery made definite sense to Lewis, who had considerable difficulty all day treating Hebe as he did his usual models. He'd been hesitant to ask her to strip, which quite threw him off. After finding her glove, he'd decided to discover more about her, and when he recalled her address was on the note she'd sent him inquiring about the position, he decided to do something about it. Once he'd discovered the paper where he'd tossed it among the pile of books on the table, he'd sent for his carriage.

Lewis's thoughts returned to the present when his carriage stopped outside a handsome mansion, the residence of Lord and Lady de Lacy. Lewis climbed the steps to raise the knocker. The butler, Wheatcroft, opened the door and greeted him warmly as an attractive dark-haired lady rushed down the stairs.

"Lewis!" His sister kissed his cheek, greeting him as if she hadn't seen him in months instead of dining with him last Saturday. Drawn into the splendid comfort of the de Lacy's small salon he soon learned that his opinion was required concerning their cousin's recent appalling behavior with Lady George at the Lambton's ball.

"... and then Cousin Gilbert had the temerity to ask me to mind my own affairs while he would take care of his," Emmy finished up, handing Lewis a cup and saucer painted with flowers.

"Mm. Always was a bit forthright, Gilbert." Still thinking of Hebe, Lewis had lost the thread, and fearing he'd be asked for his opinion on something he'd missed during Emmy's account, sought to distract her. "Have you come across a family by the name of Fenchurch?"

Emmy widened her large brown eyes. "Why, yes." She tapped her chin with a finger. "Now, wasn't a lord by the name of Fenchurch involved in some frightful scandal? I believe he was. Colin told me something of it. There was talk at his club." She picked up a shortbread biscuit and took a bite.

"A scandal?" Lewis patiently sipped his tea while she dabbed at the crumbs on her lips with her napkin.

"Colin is a remarkable font of knowledge, but I suspect he filters it for my ears." She huffed. "Most annoying!"

"Has my name been taken in vain?" came a deep voice from the doorway. Tall, fair-haired Lord de Lacy walked into the room, his blue eyes smiling affectionately at his wife. "Good to see you, Lewis. Are you here for the gossip?"

Emmy glared at her husband, but her visage softened into an indulgent smile. "Shall I pour you a cup of tea, darling?"

"No thank you, my love. Care for something stronger, Lewis? Wine, perhaps?"

"I'm afraid your excellent vintage would be lost on me. My palate is spoiled," Lewis said with a grin.

"Well, you might have said." Emmy believed that every ill was cured with a cup of tea. She turned to her husband who had settled beside her on the blue damask sofa. "Do you recall the scandal that involved the Fenchurch family?"

Colin took a sandwich from the platter. "I do. I gather you refer to Adrian Fenchurch, Baron Forth. Forth, had become embroiled in a swindle involving the East India Company. He was subsequently charged with fraud. Shot himself before he faced trial. However, I suspect the poor fellow may have been set up by others to take the blame."

"That's where I heard the name," Lewis said with a nod. "What happened to his family?"

"Lady Forth and her daughter were victimized in the most appalling fashion. Family turned their backs on them."

So that was it, Lewis thought, choosing an egg and cress sandwich smelling faintly of mustard. "They now reside in Cheapside."

"Oh, the poor things. As I recall their daughter was making her debut. She is very pretty. I quite liked her." Emmy poured Lewis another cup despite him shaking his head to dissuade her. Brown eyes much like his gazed at him. "How do you know they live in Cheapside?"

"Someone mentioned them, and I wondered, that's all."

Emmy frowned. "Oh! I don't believe you, Lewis. You know more, and you won't tell me."

"Emmeline." Colin used an authoritative voice one seldom heard. "That is tantamount to calling your brother a liar. And it cannot be substantiated."

Emmy firmed her lips. "We are not in a court of law, my lord eminent barrister, and I am not a defendant."

Colin laughed. "Are you using my profession against me? Perhaps you should become one."

"That will be the day when a woman barrister can enter a courtroom and practice law," she said crisply. Her bright gaze settled on her brother once more. "If I ask nicely, will you tell me?"

"I will not, Emmy. I often move in different circles to you as you well know."

"And I must say your circles are infinitely more interesting."

Lewis and Colin laughed.

"Are you attending the Mulgrave's card party next Saturday?" Emmy asked. "A lady I should like you to meet will be there."

Lewis sighed. He couldn't tell Emmy about his true relationship with Hebe, for fear of upsetting Colin. Even though Emmy would have handled the knowledge with aplomb. Extremely protective since Emmy's miscarriage, Colin guarded his wife closely. It was now required of Lewis to make amends. "Of course, delighted."

Chapter Three

THE NEXT DAY in the studio, Lewis greeted Hebe with his distant smile. "Good morning, Hebe."

"Good mornin', Lewis. 'Tis brisk out." Hebe rubbed her arms and moved gratefully closer to the fire smoldering in the grate. "But nice an' warm in 'ere."

He gestured at the white silk sheet folded on the chaise. "After you undress, drape this around yourself, like so..." He indicated with a hand. "One arm and shoulder uncovered." He glanced at her top knot. "Leave your hair as it is."

Hebe hurriedly stripped off her clothes. Cocooned in the sheet, she tripped out from behind the screen with the silky fabric trailing behind her. She kicked it back with a foot and almost laughed. It reminded her of the long train she'd worn when presented at court.

With a nod of approval, Lewis approached her, the sunlight through the attic window shining on his dark head.

Hebe held her breath while he teased out a lock of her hair to rest against her neck. She stared at his broad chest, suffering an absurd urge to trace the pattern over his Egyptian-brown silk waistcoat. He smelled of starch, fresh linens, and tangy lemon soap, which was nothing like Mr. Wainscot.

After she was positioned on the chaise with her head slightly turned to the left, he stepped back to view the result. "Perfect." He studied her, a hand on his chin. "You can hold that pose?"

"I'm an old 'and at this." She held herself stiff in the pose.

Lewis shrugged on a white cloth coat and pulled on a pair of thick gloves. After holding a wooden sliding scale up to her, he marked the measurements on the stone with a pencil. Then, taking up one of the bigger chisels and a hammer, he began to knock wedges from the corners of the amorphous block of marble while Hebe watched. It was delicate work, but his hands looked strong, his fingers nimble.

Silence settled over the room, except for the tap, tap, tap, of his chisel, and the crackle of the coal fire. Careful not to move her head, Hebe's gaze took in the jumble of things on the table. She attempted to read the spines of several books on art then studied the rich patterning on a rug thrown over the chair. But her eyes constantly returned to Lewis, a picture of concentration as he bent his dark head over his work. Now pitted, the marble began to change shape beneath his chiseled attack, as the chips fell onto the sheet at his feet.

Two hours passed in relative silence. Completely absorbed, his gaze flickered over her as if she wasn't a living, breathing person, but a statue herself. Fascinated, she watched him knock out the edges of stone with a flat chisel and hammer as the rough shape of her head, neck, and shoulder, emerged.

"We'll have a break." Lewis put down the implements. He emerged from behind the marble block pulling off the gloves and strode over to pull the bell cord.

Hebe stood clutching the sheet against herself. "I'll put on my robe."

He turned his back to her and rummaged through the papers on the table. "Mm? Yes, do."

When she returned, Lewis sat on the splat-back chair inspecting his drawings. As Hebe seated herself he stood and added coal to the fire. His sharp prods with the poker sent sparks flying up the chimney. She leaned back, enjoying the warmth and silence. Four stories above the road they were high in the air, with only the birds for company. Little noise reached them from the refined streets below.

There was always a cacophony of sounds in Cheapside: neighbors calling, screaming, arguing, even coming to blows. Then there were the drunks, who laughed, sang, or wept, as they staggered along the street beneath her window. It made her so tired. She supposed it was because she wasn't yet used to the constant clamor. She'd spent much of her childhood in the quiet countryside of Wiltshire. Her chest tightened, and she tried not to reflect on the past, afraid it would make her tear up. It always upset her to think of her dog. A neighbor had promised to take good care of Rex, her red setter. Her mare, Columbine, had been sold along with her father's hunters.

Hebe sighed and told herself to stop moaning about what couldn't be changed. She listened for footsteps climbing the stairs that would herald the arrival of a hot drink and something nice to eat as she hadn't had time to have any breakfast. The truth was she didn't feel a bit like moaning. She glanced over at the handsome sculptor. What woman wouldn't want to be here in his company?

Lewis sipped his coffee, strong and slightly bitter the way he liked it, while Hebe nibbled on one of Cook's scones laden with cream and strawberry preserve, her eyes closed, and her lips curled with pleasure. A dimple at the corner of her mouth caught his eye. He must get that just right. "This is so delicious." She licked a piece of jam from her bottom lip.

He lowered his gaze to his cup, amazed at how unconscious she was of her sensuality. At times, he had to steel himself to the task in hand. He had great hopes that he could capture that quality in his statue. "The preserves come from Bath. The blackberry is my favorite, you might like to try that next."

"Oh yes, Bath," she murmured taking a sip of coffee.

"You've been to Bath? My country estate lies only twenty miles from the town."

Her blue eyes widened, and she straightened on the chaise. "No. Never set foot outside 'o London."

Lewis sighed. He wondered how long he would allow this ruse to continue. He was concerned for Hebe, and didn't wish to embarrass her, but this really served neither of them.

Trouble was, he thought, casting her a reassuring smile, if he allowed the truth to come out, he would lose his model. As things now stood, she wasn't a baron's daughter. Not as she presented herself to him. But once her noble birth was revealed, the curtain between a sculptor and his model would fall. The strict morals and etiquette that society demanded of him would change everything. And he had to admit that she could turn out to be the best model he'd ever had.

He brushed the crumbs from his lap with his napkin. "Shall we begin? The days grow shorter and I'd like to put in another couple of hours before the light goes."

Hebe put down her cup and hurried behind the screen. "You've achieved a lot already, Lewis," she called. "Shouldn't take you long, seein' as it's only to be of the 'ead and shoulders."

Lewis stared at the screen while he pulled on his coat. "This is just the beginning. It will be a full-length statue. I plan to begin the torso next week." His body stirred at the thought. He went still with horror. This had never happened before. What was wrong with him?

Just then Hebe appeared from behind the screen clutching the sheet, her eyes wide. "Oh! Yes, of course."

Her reaction surprised and sobered him. Surely she had posed naked for artists. This would mean nothing to her. "Perhaps I should have mentioned it earlier," he said fighting to sound casual, as he came to rearrange her pose.

"Not at all," she said sitting upright.

He breathed in the scent of violets, her hair silky soft beneath his fingers. There was something vulnerable about her as she clutched the sheet to her slim body. It occurred to him what his problem was. He felt compassion for her. He dropped his hand. *Because dash it all! It wasn't right.*

She was driven to do this work out of desperation, due to her circumstances, none of which was her fault. He was like the rest of them, compounding the cruelty that had been visited on her. He spun around and retreated to his block of marble, placing his hands on the hard stone while he ordered his thoughts. The coldness beneath his fingers worked to cool his ardor.

"Is there anything wrong, Lewis?" came the small anxious voice behind him.

What to do? To dismiss her would mean casting her back onto the streets. What if another job didn't come along? And dammit, he didn't want to lose her. "Nothing Hebe," he said, turning back to her, his voice tight. "Let's begin."

The ability to immerse himself in his work had never failed him before. In the past it might have been Prinny sitting there on the sofa for the dearth of attraction he felt for his models. This time, when he gazed at Hebe, he saw *her*. It made his chest tighten, and he was afraid his hand would slip. One hard jab could split the marble and ruin it.

Have a care, fool! He took another deep breath. It wasn't that Hebe was any more beautiful than other models he'd used, why even Marigold...

Suddenly, the door flew open and a curvaceous redhead in a snug gown of green satin decorated with silk camellias, rushed in like a whirlwind. "So, it's you!" She stabbed an accusatory finger at Hebe. "I 'eard 'is lordship 'ad a new model. I never expected it to be you."

Startled, Hebe stared at her. "Yes, it's me, Marigold. As you can see."

"You 'ave no right..." Marigold began.

"I heard you were posing for an artist in Holland Park. That you no longer worked here." Hebe's gaze flew to Lewis for confirmation.

"Walter Ashe isn't it?" he asked walking over to her.

Marigold nodded. "But 'e only wanted to paint me 'ands. Imagine that." She held up a hand. "Said mine were pretty."

"Hands are all he paints. I commissioned a painting for Lady Chesterton. Marigold..." Lewis took her by the arm. "What are you doing here?" It wouldn't have been Stubbs. He'd given his butler firm instructions not to admit her.

"Hebe's not right for you, Lewis." Marigold pulled away from him. "Look at 'er, she's too pale and flat chested."

Lewis turned to where Hebe stood clutching the sheet. "You'd best get dressed, Hebe. We'll finish up... begin again tomorrow."

Hebe darted behind the screen as Marigold wandered over to examine his work. She spun around with a triumphant expression. "See? You've only done 'er 'ead! She don't inspire you like I do."

Lewis rang the bell. There would be hell to pay when he found out who had admitted her to the house. "Sit down while I send for coffee. We need to talk."

Marigold nodded. Pleased, she pulled her knitted shawl of a different green around her bosom and settled her ample bottom on the chaise.

Minutes later, Hebe emerged from behind the screen, her usually neat appearance suffering somewhat from haste.

"I am sorry, Hebe. Tomorrow. Usual time," Lewis said.

Hebe nodded. "Tomorrow then. Goodbye."

After the door closed, Lewis turned to the girl. He tamped down the desire to remove her bodily from the room. "Now, Marigold..."

"Would you like me to disrobe?" She fingered the buttons on her dress with a coy smile.

God help me. Lewis shook his head. "That won't be necessary, thank you."

He drew up a chair. "Are you in need of work?"

"Course I am. What kind 'o question is that?"

"I can recommend you to a friend of mine who is at present without a model."

Marigold pouted. "I like it 'ere with you."

Lewis frowned, losing patience. "I intend to continue with Hebe. I'm not about to change."

She gave him a sly glance. "Me brother, Seth won't like it if you shove me out. You don' want to make 'im maggotty."

Lewis ran his hands through his hair. "That is a chance I'll have to take. I don't wish to shove you out, as you put it, Marigold. But after you've had your coffee and cake, I should like you to behave nicely and leave."

"An' if I don't?"

"I'll instruct the footman to remove you."

She cast him a hostile glance, huffed, and settled back on the seat. "I 'ope it's chocolate cake."

Women! More trouble than they were worth. Lewis tapped his fingers on the chair arm and considered sculpting busts of naval heroes in the future.

Chapter Four

HEBE WALKED UP the steps to her front door, dread tightening her stomach. Was she about to lose her job? Marigold was beautiful and very determined. Hebe wondered if the model had been right. Was it Lewis' opinion that her body lacked the right look for Aphrodite? Would buxom Marigold be seated on the chaise longue when Hebe arrived tomorrow?

At least, Mr. Wainscott didn't lurk in the parlor, today. She feared she might have been less than polite to him if she found him there. Her mother was out too. The house was quiet. She climbed the stairs to her bedchamber dragging her feet as if lead weights were attached to her ankles. She tidied her clothes and tried to convince herself that if needed, another job could easily be found. Failing, she sank onto the bed with a sigh. At the sound of the front door opening, she hurried down to greet her mother.

Mama smiled as Hebe took the heavy basket from her. "You're home early, dearest. Come and have something hot to drink. I indulged in some chocolate. I shouldn't have, but one must have a treat now and again. And I found the perfect blue wool for the shawl I plan to have finished before the days grow cold. We shall have to economize on heating. I never realized how expensive coal is."

As her mother chatted on, Hebe followed her to the kitchen where the cook was rolling dough, her spirits lowering further. What if she had little money to give Mama on Friday? Trawling the artist's studios again looking for work was too awful to contemplate. After tomorrow, would she ever see Lewis again? That was hardest of all. It wasn't just that she liked him, it was peaceful there, and the work was more interesting. Artists tended to be secretive about their paintings; many threw a cloth over their canvasses when the day's work was done.

The next morning, Hebe found Marigold hovering at the top of Mount Street.

"I've been lookin' out for yer," she called. "Wanted to warn yer."

Hebe frowned. "What about?"

Marigold hurried over. "Look!" She pulled back her hair and turned her face to better display the dreadful bruise on her cheek, her left eye black and swollen.

Hebe's anguished gasp breathed in Marigold's cheap scent, somehow making her even more sorry for the girl. "Oh. That's awful, Marigold. What happened?"

"Lewis hit me. A fearful temper that one." She arranged the lock of hair to better conceal the bruise. "Be careful, Hebe. If I was yer, I wouldn't work for 'im."

Hebe stared at her. "It was Lewis? Why would he do such a thing?"

"I riled 'im. Needed the work. Me ma's sick."

Hebe shook her head. Confused, she struggled to take it in. "I am sorry. What will you do now?"

"Don't know. Can't work like this can I?"

"I can lend you a little money if that will help."

"Thanks Hebe." She held out her hand. "Might stop me goin' on the streets for a bit."

Hebe drew out her purse. She dropped a few coins into Marigolds palm. It left her with barely enough for the hackney. "I wish it was more."

"Thanks, ducks." She nodded her head toward the house. "Give up on 'is dibs before it happens to yer."

Marigold hurried away up the street. Could Lewis be capable of such an act? It didn't equate with what she knew of him. But you never could be sure. Her pulse racing, she made her way up the lane to the servants' entrance, unsure of how to proceed.

Lewis turned to her as she came into the studio. "Hebe, I'm sorry about yesterday, but it won't happen again."

She studied him for any sign of guilt but found nothing different in his expression. "I just saw Marigold outside in the street."

He sighed heavily. "Did you?"

"She has a terrible bruise on her cheek and her eye."

He raised his eyebrows. "I am sorry to hear it. Did she say how it happened?"

"She said you hit her."

For a moment, Lewis just stared at her, then his brown eyes widened. "Marigold said *I* hit her?" He turned and snatched up his coat. "Wait here, Hebe," he said grimly. He threw open the door and was gone.

Hebe stared at the empty doorway while her mind whirled. Had they been lovers? Was that what this was about? She took a deep breath and walked over to study the marble block. Lewis had begun work on a small area of the statue's hair. She reached out to trace a stone lock with a finger, but instead, turned to listen for footsteps on the stairs which could bring about an end to her time here.

She heard a slow heavy tread. Lewis.

He entered the room. "She was gone. I didn't hit her, Hebe. I would never hit a woman." He stood looking down at her, his dark eyes imploring. "I hope you don't think that of me."

"No. I don't, Lewis." Hebe couldn't conceive him capable of such an act. Marigold wasn't very reliable when it came to the truth. Might she be angry with Lewis for letting her go and wanted to get back at him? Or maybe hoped to scare Hebe away? Sally might tell her more. As soon as she could Hebe would go to see her.

Lewis walked over to his work table to select his tools. "Let's begin, then, shall we?" he asked in a flat, defeated voice.

She darted behind the screen to disrobe. Who had hit Marigold? It was a savage blow, perpetrated by someone capable of extreme violence. Hebe shuddered and feared for her. It brought home to her how vulnerable they all were working for strange men. She'd been naïve to believe she could handle this dangerous world she'd stepped into. Her old life was gone, along with her reputation, and her chance for a happy marriage. Once this job was finished, would she still have the courage to continue?

In his library, Lewis poured himself a whiskey and sat down to think. If Marigold spread it about that he'd hit her, the past would be stirred up all over again. He was tired of defending himself against rumor. Damen was right, he should marry again to bring some measure of respectability and order to his life. Would a wife make his life easier? Or would he be put through hell again? He'd scrupulously avoided the intense passionate relationship he'd had with Laura and Adela for a good reason.

Tonight, Emmy planned to introduce him to a lady at the Mulgraves. He must at least open his mind to the possibility. Trouble was, every time he did, the bad memories would return, and the dark veil would fall, sending him into that wretched place again that he dreaded.

As the town clocks struck eleven, Lewis paid off the hackney and crossed the gas-lit pavement in Berkeley Square. With a nod to the liveried footmen at the door, he entered the Mulgrave's well-appointed mansion which was bursting with noise and light. He greeted the butler, handed his coat and hat to a maid, and went in search of his host and hostess. The Mulgraves were known for their hospitality and their rooms were always crowded.

He found Lord and Lady Mulgrave in the elegant drawing room lit by dancing lights from an impressive pair of French crystal chandeliers and offered his apologies for being late.

"Late or not, we are always pleased to see you, Lord Chesterton." Lady Mulgrave patted her ivory-colored locks, adorned with a quivering blue feather. "You have been missed."

Lord Mulgrave nodded in his vague manner. He failed to take note of the outrageous come-hither look his wife gave Lewis. But then he always turned a blind eye to his wife's affairs.

"I was sorry to be away from the country when your ball was held," Lewis said, determined not to encourage her. "Your parties are unrivaled in London."

Mulgrave nodded his gray head. "The Prince of Wales said he would come tonight."

"Indeed!" Lewis injected as much enthusiasm into the word as he was able. He found Prinny and his toad-eaters a boring lot for the most part. It seemed likely the Prince would attend as Isabella, Lady Hertford, a lady of middle-years and Prinny's current mistress, had just passed Lewis with a smile of greeting. "Ah. I believe I just caught sight of Lord and Lady de Lacy. I need a word. Please excuse me."

Lewis bowed, paused to greet those of his acquaintance, then made his way through the noisy throng flooding the reception and card rooms. He finally located his sister and her husband on the terrace.

"Rather cool out here, isn't it?" he asked, as the autumn breeze stirred his hair.

Oddly, Emmy was vigorously employing her fan. "The Mulgrave's rooms are always so stuffy."

"Are they? Can't say I've noticed," Lewis looked at Colin. He shrugged, then cast a questioning glance at his wife.

"Why would you? When you hardly ever come to these affairs," Emmy said in an accusatory voice.

"That's true." He wondered what bee had got into her bonnet. Unlike Emmy to be so disagreeable, especially where they might be overheard. What had happened to make her so? Colin appeared as baffled as he.

Emmy craned her neck. "Oh, there she is. I feared she might not come. I arranged to meet her here. It's impossible to find anyone inside." She smiled in the direction of a lady in indigo moiré silk, who had just appeared on the terrace.

Emmy rose. She hurried over and slipped her arm through the attractive brunette's and drew her to Lewis's side.

"Lady Sylvia, I should like to introduce my brother, Lord Chesterton," Emmy said, brown eyes shining. "Lewis, this is Lady Sylvia Standish."

He bowed. "Lady Sylvia."

She curtsied as her hazel eyes met his with a smile. "Lady De Lacy has been singing your praises, Lord Chesterton."

He grinned at Emmy who was smiling like a cat at the cream jug. "A biased opinion, I fear."

His sister huffed good naturedly and left them.

Lewis discreetly observed the tall, slim widow, liking what he saw. Not one of those vacuous debutantes who clung on his arm and giggled or gazed at him as if he was Bluebeard. "Are you keen to play whist or faro, Lady Sylvia?" he asked as they strolled back inside.

"Neither, but I daresay I shall before the evening is out. Please don't let me keep you from your game."

"I would prefer to talk." Lewis smiled and offered her his arm. "I spy two chairs in the corner near the potted ferns. Shall we?"

"I should like to, thank you."

"I was deeply sorry to hear of your husband's death. He and I were at Oxford together," Lewis said, after they were seated.

She raised her eyebrows. "I'm surprised we've never met."

"My work tends to consume a lot of my time. So much so of late that I fear I've begun to lack the social graces."

She smiled. "I don't believe that. I have seen your latest sculpture. It's quite marvelous."

"Thank you." Lewis removed two glasses of champagne from the footman's tray. He handed one to her. "Tell me about yourself."

"I'm afraid I'm not particularly interesting. I've been living quietly for the past year since Peter died. In fact," she hesitated, "This is the first time I've ventured into society." She laughed. "And I might not have come tonight, but for your sister. Lady Emmeline was determined that we should meet."

Lewis smiled. "My sister has exquisite taste."

A flush warmed Lady Sylvia's cheek. "You are most kind."

"Merely honest."

Lewis glanced over to where Emmy talked to a dowager. Something had stirred her to make another attempt to draw him back into society. He thought she'd come to accept his preference for an uncomplicated life. He'd hoped all that was behind them, his failed marriage, and how that had affected her, causing her to lose her baby.

"I was saddened to learn of your wife's tragic death." Lady Sylvia's words pulled him back. "Peter and I were in France when it happened."

Lewis nodded. "Some years ago, now."

"Yes. Indeed. Time passes, and heals, it's said."

"Time might not heal completely, but does soften the ache of loss," he said, more for her benefit than his.

She nodded sadly. "Peter died after a prolonged illness. One has time to prepare. But for you it must have been a terrible shock."

It was an invitation to pursue it. Her curiosity was understandable, Lewis supposed, but he had no intention of discussing the past with her. "Would we feel better if we spoke of happier things?"

She placed a hand to her bodice trimmed with black lace. "Oh, yes. I apologize. My first social engagement and you, poor man, must wish me gone."

"I would never wish to lose a lovely lady's company." Lewis took her empty glass and placed it on the table. "Shall we distract ourselves by watching a game of whist? It may tempt you to play a hand."

"An excellent idea." She accompanied him into the card room.

A crowd three deep gathered around the hazard table. A lot of money was wagered, and a rumble passed through the crowd with every roll of the dice.

Lewis and Lady Sylvia joined the observers.

A player guessed the right number, and a cheer went up.

A group of Whig politicians were standing nearby, their eyes on the game, talking quietly together. One was Laura's brother, Michael Somerville, and his crony, Nicholas, Lord Thorn, a hot-blooded, unpredictable man. The third, Basil, Lord Osborne, a solidly built, dark-haired man, Lewis only knew by sight. They made a show of turning their backs on Lewis and moved away.

Some hours later as he waited in the entry hall for his coat and hat, Somerville appeared.

"Misplaced your lackey, Somerville?" Lewis asked.

Michael's eyes narrowed with dislike. "Are you considering marrying again? I imagine you barely give a thought to Laura lying in her grave."

"Then you are wrong."

Somerville cocked an eyebrow. "I guess she grew tired of you sleeping with your models. And in the same house!"

Lewis didn't respond. Useless to deny it, the man was convinced. "I shan't discuss Laura with you, now or ever."

Cold green eyes so like Laura's assessed him. "Because you're ashamed."

"I am bitterly sorry, Michael, rather than ashamed."

Somerville shook his dark head, turned, and left the hall.

A moment later, Emmy came to find him.

"Was that Michael Somerville I saw striding away down the corridor?"

"It was."

"He refuses to accept the truth about his sister. I could tell him a thing or two."

Lewis placed a hand on her arm. "Leave it alone, Emmy, please."

"Very well. What do you think of Lady Sylvia?"

"She's a lovely woman. A lovely sad woman."

"You could make her happy, if you cared to."

"But I don't care to, Emmy. And I'm not at all sure that I could." Lewis thanked the maid who brought his things. She bobbed and left the hall. At the door, a footman stood waiting.

Emmy frowned. "You are so vexing, Lewis," she said in an undertone, holding his hat and gloves as he put on his coat. "Sylvia is interested in the arts. You would be perfectly suited."

Lewis drew on his gloves. "I knew her husband although he wasn't a particular friend. We were at university together."

"I never met him. What was he like?"

"A studious, quiet fellow. Obviously, a devoted husband. I would make a very poor replacement." He settled his hat on his head. "And pray tell why I must suddenly become a respectable married man?"

Emmy flushed. "Because you are about to become an uncle..." Her eyes widened, and she put a hand to her mouth.

Lewis drew in a breath. "Emmy! You're going to have a baby?"

She nodded with a tremulous smile, then turned to glance at the corridor leading to the drawing room.

"And you haven't told Colin, yet," Lewis said.

She looked stricken. "I plan to tell him tomorrow. It's our second wedding anniversary."

"Goose," he said with a soft stroke of her arm. "Do as you plan. And not a word about telling me first."

"Yes, I will. I don't suppose you'll reconsider about Sylvia?"

"I am sorry, Emmy. It wouldn't work. I think in your heart of hearts you know that."

She sighed. "Oh, Lewis. I do want to see you as happy as we are. With children of your own."

"At thirty I am hardly in my dotage."

Colin strode in the entry hall.

"Here comes your husband, and he's frowning."

"Poor Colin. I left him with the Dowager Lady Sinclair. She has a tender for him, you know."

Lewis grinned.

"Emmy, how could you go off like that," Colin said looking annoyed. "I just spent the last twenty minutes searching for you." He turned to Lewis. "You off, Lewis? How about a game of billiards at White's on Friday?"

"Count me in. Now I shall leave you two to sort out your differences. I intend to seek my bed."

"Which is where we are going after we locate our host and hostess," Colin said sternly.

Emmy tucked her hand in the crook of his elbow and smiled up at him. "I believe I last saw them in the conservatory."

"Goodnight, Lewis," Emmy called as Colin swept her away.

The weary footman opened the door, and with a nod of thanks, Lewis stepped out into the cold night air. He hailed a passing hackney, sank onto the hard leather squabs, and turned his mind to those warm languid days he'd spent in Greece.

An hour later, after he'd dismissed his valet, Lewis settled in bed. He blew out the candle and stared into the dark, his mind too disturbed for sleep. The few hours before dawn were always the worst time for those with   a   troubled   conscience.

Chapter Five

THE NEXT FEW days passed as they settled into a routine. Although the marble representation of Hebe's face, head and shoulders were still only rough-hewn stone, she marveled at how under his clever hands; the shapes began to take form. It was quite magical. On Friday morning she felt enough at ease with him to mention it.

"Too early to tell, but I have a good feeling about it." He raised his head to glance at her with a smile, then turned back to his work. "I have an excellent model."

His praise made her inordinately pleased. Was he just being agreeable, or did he mean it? It had required little effort on her part, but the next phase could be more challenging. Disrobing before him had become a disturbing weight on her shoulders. She found him most professional and had no reason to feel that way. And yet, especially after Marigold's comments, she feared to see disappointment in his eyes.

In the afternoon, Lewis gave Hebe her wages, which were extremely generous. She paused in the mews to count it again. Far more than any of her painters had paid her. She looked up at the house for a moment to the attic outlined against the sky. She would not see Lewis again until Monday and would miss coming here. But she had two whole days to spend with her mother with money in her purse. Where would Mama like to go? They might hire a carriage and travel into the country to take luncheon at an inn. Hebe could hardly wait to ask her. But first, she must see Sally. She'd been putting it off, not wishing to raise the unpleasantness of Marigold's accusation again.

In the narrow lanes of the East End, she entered the reeking alley which led to the garret where Sally lived with her painter. Hebe climbed the stairs and knocked on the door at the top.

"Hebe!" Sally drew her into the room where canvasses and strong smelling tubes of paint were scattered about. A covered painting perched on the easel. "Elias has just gone out. I'll make us some tea and we can have a good natter." She hesitated, and her pretty face formed a frown. "There's something I must tell you."

"Oh?" Cold fingers climbed Hebe's spine.

They sat together in the tiny living area divided from the studio by the curtain. A pot of boiling water was suspended over the coal fire. Sally made the tea and poured milk into the cups. While keeping the chipped one for herself, she handed the other to Hebe.

"Is it about Marigold?" Hebe asked.

Sally nodded. "She came to see me."

"I saw the bruises," Hebe said. "Told me Lord Chesterton struck her."

Doubt filled Sally's eyes. "According to Marigold, t'was because she refused to go to bed with 'im."

Hebe put down the cup with a startled intake of breath. "That's it then. I can't work for him."

"'ave some sense, girl," Sally said dismissively. "Marigold wouldn't refuse a lord's advances. A 'andsome one at that! And my Elias 'eard different."

Hebe sagged against the back of the wooden chair. "What?"

"It was Seth, Marigold's brother who punched 'er. A friend of Elias' said 'e's done it before."

Hope struggled in Hebe's breast. "Are you sure?"

"Seth is a member of a London gang of cutthroats. Marigold gives 'im every penny she earns. And when she doesn't get work 'e turns nasty."

"Poor Marigold." Hebe paused to consider the new information. It was certainly plausible. "I couldn't believe it was Lewis."

"Lewis is it?" Sally widened her eyes. "You fallen for 'im?"

"No of course not. But he seems a decent gentleman."

"It wouldn't be wrong for you two to get together," Sally said brightening. "After all, you both come from the same world."

"I am no longer a part of that world, Sally," Hebe said crisply.

Sally shrugged. "Sorry love. Try a coconut biscuit. Me ma made 'em. She's cook for Mr. Thrup."

Hebe took one and bit into it, savoring the sweetness. "They're delicious. Has Marigold been back to see you since?"

Sally shook her head. "No one's seen 'er around. She might've taken off somewhere until the bruising goes."

Hebe sipped the weak brew. "How beastly to have such a rotten brother."

Sally took another biscuit as the door opened. "Here's me fella back again."

Hebe finished the last of the tea. She stood and pecked Sally's cheek. "I'll come again soon."

"Don't leave it too long, love."

With a nod to Elias, Hebe left the studio. If Marigold was part of the murky London underworld, Hebe feared for her, but the model was wrong to have lied about Lewis. It surprised Hebe that in such a short time, she'd come to know him. He wasn't a violent man.

Fortunately, except for Colin and Lewis, the billiard room at White's was deserted. Colin was unlike himself tonight. Lewis hid a smile as his brother-in-law missed another shot, sending the ball into the cushion wide of its mark. His brother-in-law was usually cool and rational. Attributes that would serve him well in a courtroom. But something had happened to throw him off his game. Lewis knew what that was. He took a sip of claret and waited to be told.

"Dash it, sorry." Colin tossed down his cue. "Perhaps we should switch to cards."

"In your present mood cards might prove expensive," Lewis observed with a grin.

A smile lifted the corner of Colin's mouth. "You're probably right. I had planned for Emmy to tell you, but... dash it all, I can't keep it to myself." He clapped a hand on Lewis back. "I'm to be a father, Lewis! You're going to be an uncle."

Lewis responded with a show of surprise and delight. The delight was real. Emmy was to be a mother!

It was as if something had righted itself after the sadness. Although there was eight years between them, they'd always been close. After their parents died, Lewis had become Emmy's guardian and kept a strict eye out for rakes during her first Season. She'd married Colin soon afterward. Relieved that she'd chosen a good man, Lewis had no trouble relinquishing his authority to him. Despite her tender years, and her own sad loss, when Lewis' life fell apart two years ago, Emmy was there for him. "We must celebrate. I'll send for champagne." Lewis turned to look for a waiter.

"No. Best let Emmy tell you, herself."

Lewis smothered a smile. "The condition suits Emmy I must say. She was positively blooming at the Mulgraves."

Colin's forehead broke into a worried frown. "I pray she remains so."

"No reason she shouldn't," Lewis said, keeping his voice light. *Please God, let everything go well this time.* "Shall we visit the card room and watch the play? There's always a few amusing on-dits, despite Brummel's absence."

"Unless some daft young fellow has lost his shirt and a good deal besides," Colin said as he followed him out.

Some hours later, when Lewis sat alone in the club library nursing a glass of whiskey, Nicholas Thorn entered. "Alone, Chesterton?" he drawled.

"I was. And hope to be again," Lewis said, pointedly fluttering the journal in his hands.

Thorn shrugged his big shoulders. Not a handsome man by any stretch, his features blunt, but Lewis had seen him turn on the charm when a lady was involved. Tonight he seemed to be spoiling for a fight. Perhaps his present mood came from the fact that his father had threatened to disinherit him due to his son's refusal to toe the line.

"Saw an amusing caricature of you in a print shop window," Thorn said, his thin lips pulled into a rictus-like grin. "Drawn as Pan with a chisel in one hand having your way with your latest sculpture. Diana the huntress, wasn't it?"

"Small things amuse the smallest of minds they say," Lewis commented returning to the article he'd been reading.

"They did not draw you small you'll be pleased to hear," Thorn said. "But then these cartoonists tend to exaggerate. We have only to ask your models."

Lewis had had enough. "Be careful, Thorn. If we were to meet in Potter's Field at dawn, I would draw your cork. Then your father would hear of it and he is ready to disown you, I hear."

Thorn swore volubly and left the room.

Lewis spent the next two days in the studio working hard. The filing and smoothing that would tease the beauty from the stone would come later, but he was now ready to move ahead. He had advised Hebe of it, but when she entered his studio on Monday morning, she appeared subdued, and avoided his gaze. He thought of suggesting a glass of wine, he rather needed one himself, but dismissed the idea. Better to offer her something to eat. He doubted she ate breakfast.

As they sat with their muffins and coffee a knock sounded at the door. "Come." The servants wouldn't interrupt his work unless it was something serious.

His butler puffed as he entered the room. Lewis stared at him in surprise. Stubbs never came upstairs. "A note has been delivered, milord. From a Mr. Crabbe."

"Couldn't it have waited?"

"I didn't like the cut of the fellow's jib, milord," Stubbs said. "Threatening manner he had. Thought it better not to delay."

Lewis perched on the edge of the table and scanned the note. "Someone called Seth Crabbe is demanding to be told where his sister, Marigold is. He believes I have hidden her away."

Hebe put down her cup. "If I knew where she was I wouldn't tell him. Seth knocks her about when she doesn't 'ave money to give 'im."

"Tell the fellow we don't know, Stubbs."

"Very well, milord."

When the door closed on the butler, Lewis crumpled the note into a ball. He eased off the table while admitting to himself that he was in some way to blame for the girl's plight even though she'd found work after he let her go. This was becoming complicated. He didn't want the girl drawing gossip down on his head and involving Hebe. "Do you have any idea where she might be?"

"Marigold 'as two friends in the business, Dora, and Liza. One of 'em might 'ave put her up."

"Shall we go and see?"

Surprise widened her eyes, but she popped the last piece of muffin in her mouth and stood.

As Lewis drove his curricle out of the stable mews behind his townhouse, Seth Crabbe pushed himself off a wall and strode over to them. A big, burly fellow with red hair, he glowered at them and grabbed the horses' reins. "You know where Marigold is, don't you, Miss Hebe?"

Lewis raised his whip. "Unhand the horses, sir."

Seth held up both hands and backed away.

"I don't," Hebe said. "And I wouldn't tell you if I did. You blackened Marigold's eye." She glared at Seth as Lewis told the horses to walk on.

Seth turned to follow as they drove past him. "What if I did? She had it coming," he spat.

"Poor Marigold," Hebe said.

"Indeed," Lewis said in a grim tone.

"What will you do if you find her?" Hebe asked Lewis as he drove them through the squalid East End streets.

"I'll send Marigold to my Bath estate if she agrees. She'll be safe there." He smiled at Hebe. "Who knows? Maybe she'll want to remain in the country." He doubted it. A London girl would miss the hustle and bustle of the big city.

"That is generous of you, Lewis," Hebe said. "Especially when Marigold said such dreadful things about you."

Lewis shrugged. "We're all capable of behaving badly when we're in trouble." He glanced at her. "We might try the artist Walter Ashe. He may be using Marigold again."

He turned the horses' heads toward Holland Park.

They negotiated the traffic and reached the treed streets of Holland Park within the hour. Ashe's house was a two story brick set in a tidy garden with a studio tacked on one side. The artist, a short man his hair graying at the temples, struggled to open the front door, his right hand bandaged.

Lewis introduced them.

"Lost my maid at the worst time. Have to do for myself." Ashe held his hand up. "Darndest thing. Cut my palm peeling an apple." He led them into a large studio with floor to ceiling windows along one wall and a glass skylight.

Hebe stared around apparently spellbound. The other three walls were hung with large oil paintings, all of which were of hands.

"Excellent light," Lewis said approvingly.

"Yes. I'm eager to make use of it and find this injury most annoying," Ashe said. "We've met haven't we, milord?"

"You painted Lady Chesterton's hands."

Ashe's hazel eyes went hazy as if in thought. "But of course, I remember the lady. You're not here to buy a painting then? What can I do for you?"

"I'm inquiring about a model, Miss Marigold Crabbe, I believe you've employed her in the past."

"Marigold?" Ashe nodded. "I was working with her." He drew a cover away from a canvas resting on an easel. It was a half-finished painting of a pair of well-shaped hands. He shook his head with a frown. "Couldn't continue after this happened, so I paid her and sent her off yesterday."

"Did she tell you her direction?" Hebe asked.

Ashe studied her. "You're a model?"

"Yes. I work for Lord Chesterton."

"Ah yes. Sculpture. An interesting medium." Ashe shook his head. "Haven't a clue where young Marigold was off to. Might be anywhere. She's a tempestuous young lady."

When they left the house, Hebe frowned at him.

"What?" Lewis asked, as he assisted her into the curricle.

"His eyes looked strange. They were cloudy, the irises enlarged."

"That would be from Absinthe. Some artists use it. They say it improves their work."

"I don't see how it could," Hebe said with a shake of her head. "He didn't even ask why we wanted Marigold." She settled in the curricle beside him. "And we're no closer to discovering where she might be."

"We'll try a couple of painters I know."

Some hours later, after visiting Marigold's mother, and another of her model friends, which proved a dead end, they were forced to give up. Marigold wasn't to be found, and gunpowder gray clouds had rolled in across the sky turning the day to night.

"That's it for today then," Lewis said. "Can't work in this light. Shall we stop at an inn for luncheon? And then I'll drive you home."

"No need for that." Hebe looked alarmed. "I can find my way."

"But I shan't allow it."

In the snug dining room, Lewis ordered wine, and chicken soup for them both. Hebe shifted in her seat and looked around several times.

"No one is likely to recognize you here," he said.

Her blue eyes met his. "You are so very kind, Lord Chesterton," she said, her voice soft. "I have been dishonest. I must set things to rights."

Lewis noted how she addressed him and the change in her speech, with a lowering of spirits. She was going to confess. He'd noted how she'd struggled to uphold her ruse as they'd driven around London. He'd been foolish to have suggested trying to find Marigold. Wasn't sure why he did. It was as if he had to prove to Hebe that he was a decent fellow after all. Dammit, now he would lose her. "Do you want to talk about it, Hebe?"

She raised her eyebrows her blue eyes flashing in outrage. "How long have you known?"

"That you're a baron's daughter? Not immediately. I suppose when I returned your glove and heard your mother's voice."

She firmed her mouth as the steaming plates were placed before them along with crusty bread from the oven, warm and yeasty, with fresh butter.

When they were alone again, Hebe took several sips of burgundy. Her blue eyes had become shadowed. "Why did you allow me to continue to make a fool of myself?"

"You did no such thing. You're a good model so naturally, I wished to keep you. I'm a selfish man, Hebe. My aim was to finish the statue."

"You could have hired someone else."

"You were my inspiration for Aphrodite."

"I was?" Her cheeks flushed pink.

He smiled. "You, and a mosaic of the goddess I discovered in Greece." He refrained from adding what part of their body inspired him most.

"Whether you are aware of the truth or not makes little difference, surely," she said.

"But it does, Hebe." He noted the worry in her eyes. "I am guilty of ignoring your circumstances. It was wrong from the start. I understand your need to work, but I would prefer to help you find more acceptable employment."

"Don't you think I've tried?"

She looked so crestfallen, his heart went out to her. He disliked the idea of her working at all. "Please allow me to help you."

"Thank you, Lewis. I appreciate the offer more than I can say. But now I will finish this tasty meal and go home." She ducked her head, hiding her expression and took a piece of bread from the plate.

Lewis was absurdly downhearted. It wasn't that he'd lose a good model. He would miss her. It had been remarkably pleasant to have a lady of her quality working for him. But he'd balked at seeing her stripped naked, he had to admit. It seemed like a dreadful invasion of this lovely young woman's privacy. It probably wouldn't have worked if he'd continued.

They ate in silence, Lewis having given up after Hebe's monosyllabic replies to his attempt at conversation.

When they'd finished, Lewis paid the bill, helped Hebe into her pelisse and they left the coaching inn, crossing to where a servant had been holding the horses.

"Miss Hebe Fenchurch? Can that be you?" A young lady in a moss green pelisse and matching bonnet hurried toward them along the footpath.

Hebe turned her stricken face to him. "It's Lady Felicity Merton, we met during my London Season."

Lewis glanced over at the small, carrot-haired young woman advancing smartly along the street. "Then introduce me."

"How nice to see you," Felicity said, a little short of breath. Her maid had trailed along behind her and now stood nearby. "I'd just visited the apothecary for Mama's medicine and I said to Maisie, that I was sure it was you." Her curious gaze flicked over Lewis. "Many have wondered whether you and your mother had left London, after your poor papa died. We thought you might have gone to live with your grandfather at his estate in Kent."

"Lady Felicity, may I introduce you to Lord Chesterton? He is a friend of my mother's and has kindly offered me a lift this morning."

Felicity bobbed. "How do you do, Lord Chesterton."

Lewis bowed. "Lady Felicity."

"We haven't seen you anywhere this Season, Hebe." Curiosity was writ large on Felicity's face. She glanced at Hebe's drab pelisse. "Perhaps we will, now that your mourning period has passed?"

"My mother and I have been away from London."

"Oh. During the Season? You have missed many delightful engagements." She rattled off the names of two: a ball and a dance party. "And all the gossip at

Almack's! I can't wait to tell you about Annabella Crawley!"

Lewis glanced at the sky. "I believe it is about to rain. Please do excuse us, Lady Felicity. My horses are growing restive."

"I believe you are right, my lord." She smiled at him as if he'd pronounced something of great magnitude and shook out her umbrella. "Shall we see you at the Iverson's rout, Hebe? We can catch up then."

"I don't expect to as Mama has been a trifle under the weather."

"You really should have her try Mr. Blanchard's tonic." Felicity's maid obligingly held up the bottle. "It's known to be strengthening."

"What an excellent idea. I shall tell her. Thank you, Felicity. Good day." Hebe put her hand on Lewis' arm and climbed into the curricle.

As the horses drew away, Felicity stood watching them.

"It seems I'm always telling lies. I should not have said that about my mother," she said gloomily.

Lewis swore under his breath. "What a fool I am. I have compromised you, Hebe."

"What nonsense, Lewis," Hebe said, straightening her hat. "It is not scandalous to be seen in a carriage with a gentleman. Especially if he is a friend of the family. Please don't give it another thought."

He glanced at her, marveling that she thought of him rather than herself, then turned to guide the horses around a wagon piled high with vegetables. "I am immune to gossip. But I hope this doesn't rebound on you."

She raised her chin. "I don't see how it could as I am not part of that world now."

Hebe's forced smile sent a streak of protectiveness through him. Aware of her fierce determination to hang onto her pride, he had to tread carefully. He pulled the horses up farther along the street from her house and reached for his wallet. "I usually give my models a bonus when I finish a work."

"But it's not finished."

"The most important part of it is. The head and shoulders. I have my drawings to help me complete the rest." It wasn't entirely true. He was sure that nothing in his imagination could do justice to Hebe naked. He removed a bundle of bank notes and held it out to her.

Her gaze flew to his. "That's too generous. There's no need, I'm sure to find work."

Lewis opened her gloved hand and pressed the money into it. "Don't be foolish. Your mother will appreciate it."

"Oh, yes. She will. Thank you for everything, Lewis. You've been so very good to me."

He tied off the reins and jumped down. She took his arm, and they walked along the street. When they approached her house, he bowed his head and left her.

Seated on his curricle, he waited until she slipped inside. As his gaze lingered on the shut door, he suffered a strange sense of loss. A tightening of his ribs. He shrugged and moved the horses on with the damning sensation that he'd let her down. That he hadn't done enough. He feared he would continue to worry about her, that it wouldn't be a case of 'out of sight, out of mind' as Chaucer had put it.

Chapter Six

WHEN HEBE GAINED her bedchamber, she sank onto the bed. It hurt terribly that she would never see Lewis again, never watch him work, his tall, lean frame bent over the marble. She'd grown familiar with his gestures, the way he smoothed back his thick black hair, and gave her all his attention when he'd stopped work to join her for luncheon.

It had been good of him to offer to help her. But he'd been so generous already. It was enough to know that he would help, should she go to him. Hebe had doubted she would ever put her faith and trust in another man. Not after her father had left them in such dreadful straits. But Lewis had restored her faith. It was hard to bear that she had lied to him. He had known all along! And he'd said nothing, while she continued to make a fool of herself.

She took a deep breath and counted the money. *Eighty pounds!* It would stand them in good stead for some months and give her time to find work. She could continue to give her mother a weekly allowance without her realizing that Hebe had lost her job. She sat back and frowned. Lewis had given her far too much. Was it out of sympathy? The thought horrified her. She would have to find a way to repay most of it. But right now, she was in no position to.

Hebe sagged at the thought of venturing out in search of work again. Hopefully, one of the artists she'd worked for might need her for a new painting. She would troll the studios tomorrow although nothing would induce her to return to Alberto Bertoletti.

Fresh worries now assailed her, and her confidence waned. She had been careful never to venture into parts of London where the *ton* might go. And her artists, apart from Lewis and Sally, did not know her full name. What if someone else recognized her? And discovered the truth? The shock really would make her mother ill. Poor Mama. After Papa died, the invitations had dried up, and it became impossible to make morning calls or indeed receive them. Her mother refused to show her face anywhere. The family had fallen so far from grace it appeared that the polite world had forgotten them. But apparently, according to Felicity, they hadn't.

Her mother came into the room. "Mr. Wainscott called in today."

Hebe swallowed her throat suddenly dry. "What did he want?"

"To inform me that he is about to be married. He was concerned because he had asked you first, Hebe, which you failed to mention to me." Mama paused and raised her eyebrows. "After he received no reply, he decided it best to choose another lady."

"I am sorry, Mama. I'd forgotten all about it." Hebe's guilt was heavily laced with relief. "I wouldn't have accepted him."

Her mother sighed. "I fear you might have done so just to please me. But I very much doubt I would have let you."

Hebe went hot with relief. "You didn't want me to marry him, Mama?"

"Wainscott is not good enough for you, my dear. And I will never allow you to become a sacrificial lamb." She took Hebe's arm. "Come into the parlor. I wish to talk to you."

When they settled on the sofa, Mama took up her knitting. "As you know I have written to your grandfather again but have yet to receive a reply. I am concerned that his reason for abandoning us was due to his financial situation. I should like to talk to him as I remain hopeful that he might suffer some guilt for his actions."

Hebe remained doubtful. "I know you do, Mama."

"A letter has come, however, from your father's spinster sister, Aunt Prudence, in East Sussex."

"After all this time?"

"The few times we met she was never particularly warm toward me, quite indifferent in fact. But it appears that she has a good opinion of you, Hebe."

"I don't see why she should. We hardly know each other." Hebe was surprised, having only seen her aunt once, some years ago at Christmas at Longford House, Grandfather's estate, when she was sixteen. Her impression of her aunt was of a vague lady who had wafted about in trailing draperies and possessed consuming interests in bees, the cosmos, and her yappy terrier with the unlikely name of Aries.

"Prudence has written to tell me she needs a companion and, as the stars are in alignment, you might do."

Her dreams of independence faded. Hebe drew in a breath and released it slowly grappling with the awful prospect of living in a small village in East Sussex with her eccentric Aunt. "Will you come too, Mama?" Her voice sounded surprisingly calm; when she wanted to scream and rail at the unfairness of life.

"For a short while, and then I shall visit your grandfather. I hope to receive a small stipend from him which will keep me for the years I have remaining on this earth. I believe it is his duty. Hopefully he has come to realize it."

"Why does Grandfather blame us for Papa's death? We did nothing to cause it."

"He disliked your father's choice of bride, Hebe. He considered me too meek. At the funeral he suggested that a stronger woman would have kept your father in line."

"That's so unfair!"

"Nevertheless, he did express that view. Of course, he was grief-stricken. His only son. Suicide is a dreadful blight on a proud family like the Fenchurch's."

"He is hateful," Hebe said fiercely. "He left us to starve. I'll never forgive him!"

"We might have to, dear. More than a year has passed. He may have gained a better sense of proportion and will seek to right a wrong. I live in hope that he will soften and take you to his heart. You are his only grandchild." She put down her knitting and began to unwind wool from the ball. "Until then, I want you to be safe. Grief also made me mad for a while. I should never have allowed you to go out to work. The best place for you is with your aunt."

Perhaps it was for the best, now she no longer worked for Lewis, Hebe thought gloomily. "When are we to leave?"

"I intend to close up the house immediately. I've spoken to the servants. Cook has agreed to take another position. Kitty visited the employment agency today and was assured of work. Begin to pack, Hebe. We shall leave the day after tomorrow. We'll travel by stage coach and arrive before your aunt has second thoughts."

Unsettled, Lewis stared at the statue. He had little desire to tackle it but chose a broad file and began to smooth the roughened stone over the head and shoulders. As he worked, his thoughts rested on Hebe. What more could he do? She had turned down his offer to help her. Should he try again? A position within his household in the country? Ridiculous. She could never be a maid, and even should she become one, it would not help her mother.

He worked steadily by the light of a lamp and retired to bed long after midnight. Determined to make inroads before he needed to hire a new model, he rose at dawn and after a hearty breakfast, threw himself into his work.

In the late afternoon, he returned the file to his work table, pulled off the gloves and flexed his tired hands. While standing before the statue with a glass of claret, he inspected the work he'd done with a practiced eye. It was far from completed, but the stone appeared satin smooth and gleamed softly as the gathering dusk drew shadows over the room. More filing was needed to banish the dimples in the stone, but this part of the statue was as near to perfect as he could have wished. The stone coil of hair rested on one perfect shoulder. His gaze followed the line of Hebe's long neck and the tilt of her chin. He'd thought on first seeing her that she had good bones, good proportions. Now he saw even more. An undeniable beauty, yes, but strength too. There was determination in that firm chin, and perhaps a little stubbornness too.

If only she would let him help her.

He shrugged and turned his thoughts back to his work.

As night fell, instead of the warmth of a job well done, he stood there feeling as if something had gone from the room along with the light. His inspiration. Lewis cursed under his breath. Couldn't for the life of him imagine another model sitting there on the chaise. It required Hebe here to finish it.

Lewis threw off his cloth coat and headed to his bedchamber to change for dinner, having made plans to visit his club for a game of faro. He really needed some bright company.

Later in White's library, while waiting for his friend to arrive, Lewis settled in a leather armchair nursing a glass of whiskey. He was aware of some furtive glances as he flicked though the Gentleman's Magazine then sifted through the newspapers and periodicals. Was he imagining a hostile attitude directed at him from some members? He was about to put a broadsheet down when it all suddenly became clear. Walter Ashe's name had caught his eye. The artist who had painted Laura's and Marigold's hands. Lewis quickly read the small item, hardly believing the words, his blood running cold. Ashe had been interviewed concerning a young woman who had been identified as Miss Marigold Crabbe. Her body was found near his premises in the grounds at Holland House. He had employed the deceased as a model until recently.

Lewis rose from the chair and banged the glass down spilling whisky over the table.

"Are you all right, milord?" a waiter asked rushing over.

"Some distressing news, Jenks. I apologize for the spillage." Lewis walked over to the writing table seized a quill and quickly penned a note. He handed it to Jenks who had mopped up the whiskey and was seeing to the fire. "Please give this to Lord Trevelyan when he arrives."

Lewis tipped the man and left the club. But when he reached the street, he hesitated while the chilly wind threatened to wrench off his hat, and tried to order his thoughts. He was unsure how to proceed. Marigold dead! He didn't even know how she'd died; the article had failed to provide that information. Had she died because she was desperate to find work? Alone in the night? His chest tightened. He had to learn more. First, he must speak to Hebe. But dammit it, he couldn't call on them late at night.

Late, the next afternoon, when he expected Hebe would have returned from looking for work, he took a hackney to her house, wondering how to best approach her without revealing her secret to her mother. As he left the carriage, a housemaid emerged from the front door.

Lewis hailed her, and she swiveled to stare at him.

He strode up to her. "Would Miss Hebe Fenchurch be at home?"

She put a hand to her chest. "Oh my, you startled me, sir. Her ladyship and Miss Hebe left this morning for the country."

"Do you have their address?"

"It just so happens I do, sir. Her ladyship has gone to her sister-in-law's residence." She took a piece of paper from her pocket and held it out.

"Ambrose house, Lillyvale village, East Sussex," Lewis said. "Do they plan to be away long?"

"They made no mention of returning, sir. The lease has been cancelled."

He handed her back the note. "I see. Thank you."

Relieved because Hebe was safe and in no danger from a possible murderer who might be lurking about, he returned to the waiting hackney. He tamped down a sense of disappointment that the decision of how to proceed with the statue had been made for him and entered the carriage. "Take me to Bow Street, jarvie."

The jarvie groaned. "Bow Street, milord?"

"I gather you know where it is?"

"Course I does. Not somewhere I fancy going though."

"You have something to hide from the constabulary?"

The jarvie chuckled. "Not that, sir. I tend to avoid Covent Garden. Especially at night. Had no end of trouble with the fares I've picked up around there.

Groups of gentlemen, much like y'self, no offense milord."

"None taken."

"They have me trawling the lanes while they visit the brothels in search of ladies of pleasure. Then some balk at paying the full fare."

Dusk was falling as the carriage took off. "Some hours before the street lamps are lit, and the area gets busy," Lewis observed.

"Don't matter. The area always swarms with harlots, buffoons, and all manner of rabble," he said, urging his horse along. "Swindlers, cheats, and low gamblers. Gangs of pickpockets, who'd stab yer as easy as look at yer." He sighed gustily. "Many of the pickpockets are little more than children. I can deal with them easily enough. It's when an opera dancer offers a man their favors in lieu of fare. I'm a married man."

Lewis laughed. "I'm sure you can handle yourself," he said eyeing the driver's broad shoulders.

The jarvie grunted. "Can still be taken for a ride. A few nights ago I picked up a well-dressed gentleman from around the Garden. Wanted to go home to Mayfair. The fellow, big he was, was bleeding into his cravat. Said some harlot had stabbed 'im in the neck with a broken glass after he rejected her advances. When I got 'im 'ome, the blighter made me wait an hour before he sent the fare out with a servant. And it was 'alf me bleeding fare! He lived in a big grand house. Osborne Place it was."

Lewis paused after he was set down outside Bow Street magistrate's court, Basil Osborne was another friend of his brother-in-law's with bad habits it seemed.

He straightened his shoulders and went inside determined to get to the bottom of Marigold's death.

Chapter Seven

HEBE AND HER mother began their journey from the Swan and Two Necks in Lad Lane, Cheapside, where they were made aware of the costs and the danger of being fleeced during the journey to Brighton. They would be required to pay for their meals and lodgings. How fortunate to have obtained seats inside the stage coach with a man and his wife. They pitied the eight poor souls who rode on the roof. Hebe gripped her reticule filled with sympathy for them when the coach lurched around a corner and tilted alarmingly.

After a day of unrelenting rain, a wheel became stuck in a water-filled pothole. All the passengers climbed down and waited while the horses were backed up. Hebe grew concerned for her mother, her face pinched and white beneath her umbrella. When the coach finally broke free of the mud, everyone cheered and clambered back on. The second time it happened no one cheered. Every ten miles they changed horses and took advantage of a brief stop where food and drink was available. It was hard to eat a meal when the coach took off again after twenty minutes. And they had little appetite after they learned that the uneaten food was sold again.

As the day dragged on, the man sitting opposite lit his pipe. Ignoring his wife's faint protest, he puffed away, the smoke filling the coach interior. He glared at Hebe when she coughed and took out her handkerchief.

Two uncomfortable nights passed at noisy, packed, coaching inns, and at sunrise, after a rushed breakfast, all of them climbed aboard again.

Late on the third day, the smell of the sea greeted them. The coach deposited them in bustling Brighton where her mother hired a hackney for the journey to Lady Prudence's residence some miles inland.

The driver pulled up outside a red brick two-story house, with attic windows in the slate roof, surrounded by an abundant garden. He removed their trunk, pocketed his fare, and left their luggage on the carriage drive.

Exhausted, their clothes soiled and crumpled, Hebe helped her mother up the steps wondering what kind of reception awaited them. It appeared that Lady Prudence lived simply for an earl's daughter for the property was by no means grand.

A maid in a black dress and white mobcap opened the door. She bobbed. "I'm Mary, milady. Please come in, yer expected."

As they entered the hall, a cacophony of shrill barking sounded from within. The terrier, Aries, a little older and fatter than Hebe remembered, rounded a corner at speed on his short legs. He ran straight for her and launched himself into her arms.

Hebe staggered and dropped her reticule.

The maid took little notice. She gestured toward the door. "I believe Lady Prudence is still in the garden. Quite a morning it's been. Please come into the parlor. I'll tell 'er ladyship yer 'ere."

"Our trunk?" Mama asked faintly.

"Diggory will fetch it," the maid said.

Hebe and her mother followed the maid with Aries dancing around their feet. The parlor was furnished with a mixture of uncoordinated pieces of furniture. The green velvet sofa they sat on had worn patches on the arms.

After the maid left the room, Hebe leaned down to pat the dog before he tore her stockings to shreds. "Is Lady Prudence not comfortably off?"

"I must say I find this surprising." Mama looked about with a pained expression.

At that moment, Lady Prudence entered the room dressed in a flowing round gown with a chemisette tied at her neck, a style popular before Prinny became Regent. She wore her brown hair pulled back in a severe chignon, and her hands, when she took Hebe's in a strong grip, were rough to the touch.

She gave Hebe's hands a little shake before releasing them. "Well, here you are. I planned to come and meet you at the inn, but Bertie escaped his cage and flew out of the window."

"Oh, I'm sorry," Mama said. Neither of them asked what Bertie might be. It didn't seem necessary as it was clear he must be a bird of some sort.

"The gardener climbed the oak in the end," Aunt Prudence explained with a smile of satisfaction. "We had a terrible time trying to catch him. Diggory professes to be afraid of heights. Such nonsense. My, Amelia, you do look drawn. Mary, don't stand rooted to the spot, tell Cook to make sandwiches, and..." she called as Mary made for the door, "... scones, the gooseberry preserves, cream, and don't forget the honey." She perched on the chair opposite them looking rather like some sort of odd bird herself. "My bees have been most obliging. We have put up several jars." Her hazel eyes scrutinized Hebe. "Are you interested in apiology?"

Hebe found her aunt's eyes quite penetrating. "I'm afraid I've never had much to do with bees." She sank back onto the sofa cushions as Aunt Prudence described the demands of being a beekeeper.

She let her aunt's talk flow over her. It had been an excruciating journey. Worse than Hebe envisaged. The man and his wife left them after the first day to be replaced by two elderly men. All of them too numb to talk as they rocked sickeningly over the rutted roads. She'd worried about her mother, who'd never known such a sad lack of creature comforts. It was true Mama did look drained although not a word of complaint passed her lips.

"It is so good to see you again, Prudence," Mama said, when at last, Aunt Prudence drew breath.

"The last time we met was under such sad circumstances," Aunt Prudence agreed. "Well, here you are now, and I'm glad I offered. It's a big house, why not fill the rooms? If you plan to stay for a while, that is, Amelia."

Although it wasn't an entirely gracious invitation, Hebe felt relieved that her mother had been made welcome. At least until she'd regained her strength. Hebe knew Mama was determined to throw herself on Grandfather's mercy. She feared it might result in a crippling disappointment. But then it might be better if

Mama did leave before she realized that Hebe could never be content here. A voice in her head screamed, no, no, no.

At Bow Street, Lewis spoke to Sir Robert Baker, the chief magistrate. From the Scot, he learned the details of Marigold's death. Shocked and sickened by the violence, he gave the constables the little information he had, and then left, wondering if some still doubted him. As Laura died in much the same way, he suspected they would view him with a measure of suspicion.

Lewis returned home and sat by the fire nursing a brandy. He had no desire to work, as his mind stubbornly returned to that awful period in his life when Laura had left him for the Whig Geoffrey Lancaster, son of Baron Lauderdale.

Laura and her lover had been traveling the Great North Road on the way to Geoffrey's estate in Durham. But they never reached their destination. Both were found dead in a bedchamber in the Crown Inn in Bigglesthorn, a village between St. Albans and Stilton. Robbers, it was first believed, but her jewels and possessions were not taken. Odd too that her ladyship had been strangled while Lancaster was knifed. As Lewis was on route to Bath and his country estate at the time, it was difficult to prove he hadn't been behind it. And even after an ostler and an innkeeper came forward to absolve him of any involvement, the suspicion that he might have arranged her death fueled the ton's gossip for the last two Seasons.

When Lewis visited the morgue, his heart seemed to stop beating as he gazed down on Laura's body. The image of her beautiful face ravaged in death returned to haunt him when at his weakest. He'd hired a Bow Street Runner to find the murderers. He'd even roamed the Great North Road himself, inquiring at coaching houses and the villages their coach passed through. He'd found nothing, and neither had the Runner. It remained an extraordinary and devastating mystery. Did his preoccupation with his work drive her into another man's arms? He would never be sure.

Lewis stirred from his chair, discovering the room had lightened from black to violet gray. The fire must have burned out hours ago. He shivered. Cold had seeped into his bones. A low mood had him in its grip as he rose stiffly and returned to his bedchamber. He stretched out on the bed filled with despair as he fought to find a clear way ahead. One thing was certain. He wouldn't work with another model. It was doubtful he would ever finish the statue. After an hour, he rose, washed in cold water, and dressed without calling for his valet.

In his studio, Lewis stood and faced the marble, glowing in the early morning light. It seemed to take on a life of its own. He seized a mallet and advanced on it, determined to break it into a thousand pieces.

A knock sounded at the door. "Milord?"

Lewis put the mallet back on the table. "Come in Dunston."

His valet hurried in with a reproachful expression. "I brought your shaving water to your bedchamber and discovered you'd dressed yourself, milord."

Lewis sighed. He refused to remain in the city and have people stare at him with suspicion again. He'd lose his mind. "You are to shave me, Dunston. And pack enough clothes for at least a week."

"Where is your direction, milord? If I may be so bold to ask?"

Lewis was only too familiar with Dunston's boldness. "Bath."

"Your estate, milord?" Dunston asked hopefully. "Then I am to accompany you?"

"I'll send for you should I need you." Lewis left the room refusing to acknowledge Dunston's hangdog air. He was strung so tightly, he was desperate to be alone.

At his desk in the library, he penned a note to Emmy, advising her of his decision to remove himself from London for a while. Nothing of concern, he was at pains to reassure her. Matters requiring his attention had arisen in Surrey.

An hour later, he was tooling along the road in his curricle toward Chesterton Manor, the Tudor mansion he'd inherited from his father. The trees were dressed in the colors of early spring. His horses moved in perfect unison and the fresh country air after the pollution of London lifted his spirits. Before the nagging worry returned. What to do about Hebe? Should he alert her to possible danger? Or was his own situation causing him to overreact? And if he did write to her, her mother might read the letter. He mustn't chance   it.

Chapter Eight

AFTER THE INITIAL shock, Hebe had adopted the view that she had no right to be ungrateful. Her new bedchamber was comfortable and clean, and she was well fed. That was far more than many could claim. But despite talking firmly to herself, she couldn't banish the wretchedness. It was the end of hope. A future of dreary servitude stretched ahead.

Despite the worry and danger, she'd faced in London, she had been free to make her own decisions. As her savings grew, so did the anticipation that something better awaited her around the corner.

While her mother rested, Hebe took the opportunity to pen a letter to Sally at the small desk in her bedchamber, which overlooked the back garden. They'd left London so hurriedly, she'd been unable to tell Sally they were going to Brighton. Although she would love to ask if she'd heard from Marigold, Hebe didn't want to put the burden of a reply on her friend, who wasn't proficient at writing, and the post expensive.

She finished her letter and addressed it. Outside, Aunt Prudence, surrounded by bees, and looking like some strange otherworldly creature, puffed smoke about from some apparatus while she roamed among the hives. A dark veil of net attached to her wide-brimmed hat covered her face. She wore something that resembled a man's linen coat, large gloves, and boots. Hebe quickly averted her gaze from the worrying sight.

As she considered how to send Sally's letter without her mother learning of it, Mary knocked on the door.

"Lady Prudence wishes you to come into the garden, Miss Fenchurch."

Fearing the worst, Hebe followed the maid down the stairs. They left the house and crossed the lawns. Some distance away, the gardener added more dry leaves to a smoldering pile, the smoke curling into the pale gray sky to be snatched and carried away by the cool autumn breeze. "Is that Diggory?"

"Yes, miss," Mary said. "'E's a good sort. Don't let 'is appearance worry you."

Hebe flicked another curious glance in his direction, but the hunched figure was too far away for her to discern anything unusual about him.

Her aunt advanced toward her, holding out a spare veiled hat. "Put this on, Hebe. You have nothing to fear. The smoke calms the bees. I'll show you how to collect the honeycomb."

Hebe settled the hat on her head. Her worst nightmare had come true. She would spend her life working with bees. Her aunt explained how to collect the honeycomb as she removed a frame from the hive and carefully wiped the bees away. Hebe stepped back as they swirled angrily into the air. Aunt Prudence employed some kind of implement, transferring the honeycomb to a plate before returning the frame to the hive.

Through the dark gauze which gave a new and perplexing view of the scene, she trailed after her aunt as she trudged around the hives, while the bees buzzed close to her face, appearing anything but calm and making her flinch.

Intent on following her aunt, Hebe managed to show enthusiasm and ask appropriate questions. An hour later, she was released from the suffocating net hood and followed her back to the house.

Aunt Prudence, obviously pleased with her, removed her hat, patted her hair, and smiled. "Time for tea."

"I must tell Mama."

"No, let her rest. I'll have a tray sent up."

While Bertie, a colorfully plumed parrot, swung upside down from his perch and fixed Hebe with a malevolent eye, her aunt took what appeared to be a rolled-up chart from a cupboard. When they sat together on the sofa, she spread it out on the table in front of them. She turned to Hebe with an earnest expression. "I have been studying your astrological chart. Life has been troublesome for you, which is to be expected, as you have been under the influence of Mars."

"Oh?" Hebe knew Mars to be the God of war and the son of Jupiter and Juno. Why he should influence her life was disturbing and a little intriguing. She leaned forward but gained no further knowledge from what appeared to be a confusion of astrological symbols.

"Yes. Most worrying." Aunt Prudence nodded. "And although Mars no longer rules over you, I'm afraid things are not going to improve for some time."

Despite her skepticism, Hebe's heart sank. It seemed she was ill-fated.

Her aunt patted her hand. "You mustn't despair, for Venus has entered one of her celestial homes. Unfortunately, Venus makes a strong connection with Saturn, the celestial minister in charge of imposing austerity."

"Really?" Austerity didn't sound good. Foolish to hope even for the briefest second that Venus might be the harbinger of romance. Hebe sagged back in her seat.

"However," her aunt traced a line on the chart, "The link is both supportive and harmonious. There will be an interesting development."

Hebe blinked. "What sort of development, Aunt?"

"I shall do a complete chart and advise you of what lies ahead. Best to be prepared."

Hebe couldn't visualize anything changing. Mars still hovered over her, warlike and destructive, she was sure of it.

When the maid brought the tea things in, Hebe cleared her throat. "I thought I might walk to the village, Aunt Prudence."

"What village?" Her aunt's eyebrows rose. "Brighton is too far. The nearest village is several miles away by road. If you set out over the fields, you're sure to get lost or fall afoul of the farmer's bull. Is there something you need? Something I have failed to provide?"

"No, no. I am extremely comfortable here. I have a letter I wish to post."

Her aunt seized a small gold bell on the table beside her and rang it with vigor.

The door opened, and a bulky man with coffee-colored skin and black hair hurried in. Her aunt spoke to him in an indecipherable language.

He approached Hebe and held out a very large hand, palm up.

"Give Diggory the letter. He will post it for you." Aunt Prudence prepared the tea from an exotically painted canister and added hot water to the teapot from a jug. A sweet, slightly woodsy fragrance arose with the steam.

Hebe removed the letter from her pocket, smoothed it out and gave it to him. "Thank you, Diggory."

He nodded and left the room.

"Diggory doesn't speak more than a few words of English," her aunt explained. "It is fortunate that I can converse in his language."

Hebe accepted a cup and saucer from her aunt. "How did Diggory come to be in England?"

"His life was in danger, so I brought him home with me from British Ceylon."

"You have visited Ceylon, Aunt?"

"Yes. Dimbulla, a tea-growing area. I spent three years working in a mission there. Diggory cannot go back now, not since the armed uprising in '18."

Hebe realized she knew very little about her aunt and even less about Ceylon. She wondered why her father had never told her any of this. Had her grandfather wiped his hands of his daughter because she was different?

"One does what one can," her aunt said cryptically.

It seemed to be far more than most people did. She began to observe her eccentric aunt in a new light.

In her room, her mother sat drinking her tea. "Mama, did you know that Aunt Prudence spent three years abroad? Working in a mission?"

Her mother shook her head but didn't appear surprised. "She's known as the black sheep of the family. Your father told me she doesn't get on with your grandfather, but he never said why. She was seldom at Longford House either for Christmas or family occasions."

How harsh and judgmental people could be, Hebe thought. Once you were given a label, it seemed you could never shed it.

Lewis rode into the village and spent a pleasant morning talking to the shopkeepers. While his horse was shod at the blacksmith's he ate luncheon at the big country inn beside the river and played a game of skittles. When retrieving his horse, he met his neighbors, Lord and Lady Banbridge, who invited him to dinner.

In the late afternoon, he rode out to visit his tenant farmers, and discussed the rethatching of their cottages. That evening, in the Banbridge's handsome stone mansion set in a nice park, Lewis enjoyed a good dinner and played whist with them. Their young daughter, Amy, who was making her debut made up the four. Despite the uncomfortable thought that he had a marriage minded mama living over the hill, Lewis enjoyed the company and the ride home by the light of the moon on his favorite horse, Sabre. He used to love this life, and even though he felt invigorated to be here, he acknowledged it would never be as sweet as it once was.

Tomorrow, he would meet with his gamekeeper and his steward to discuss those improvements to the tenant cottages, plus the quail shoot that was to take place during the coming month. Very necessary, he'd been assured, to cull the birds that had bred without interruption for two Seasons.

Emmy had observed that if he were to marry again, he would spend more time here, hold a hunt ball, attend the village fetes. He knew the villagers would benefit from it. He was an absent landlord for most of the year, whereas in the past, he and Laura had been in residence for most of the autumn, Christmas, and again in mid-summer. They were known for their house parties, and the social events Laura delighted in.

The next day, Lewis wandered through the rooms of the old house with its snug low beamed ceilings. It was steeped in family history with the clutter of objects collected by his father on his travels, his mother's tapestries, the splendid Eastern rugs, the Chinese porcelain, the oil paintings, and several of his favorite sculptures.

Regrettable that he had no one to enjoy it with, but he hadn't wished for company. Even though little evidence of Laura remained—her brother had demanded he be given the portrait done of her as a young woman before she married Lewis—the sadness and the sense of failure still gathered force within these walls.

At the stables he mounted his stallion, and with his two greyhounds galloping at his heels, rode out to speak with his gamekeeper, taking note of a fallen fence as he passed by.

In the coming days, Lewis' restlessness increased, and his mind returned to the unfinished business he'd left behind in London. He should destroy the statue if he didn't plan to complete it. Move on to something else. What was wrong with him? He'd never been so indecisive about his work.

After an early morning ride, he returned to the house for breakfast, and picked up his mail from the silver server in the Great Hall. Several invitations from neighbors, and one from the vicar appealing to him to attend the church fete.

He took Emmy's letter into the breakfast room and read it while he drank his coffee. She wrote that his model's death now fueled drawing room gossip. One of the more lurid scandal rags had discovered Marigold had been strangled like Laura. *It's horrible, Lewis,* Emmy added, *perhaps you should stay away for a while until some other scandal erupts to replace it. And hopefully, the murderer will soon be found.*

Emmy offered good advice, but he was greatly disturbed that she'd come to hear of it, especially, in her delicate state. Lewis was sorely tempted to return, but after giving it serious thought, he failed to see how his presence in London would change anything. In fact, it might make things worse, so he resisted the urge to meet the matter head on. Instead, Lewis and a tenant farmer dug a trench to irrigate his fields. He returned home at night exhausted enough to sleep like the dead.

Physical work might make the body tired, but he'd discovered it failed to still the mind. Hebe remained uppermost in his thoughts. It seemed unlikely that Marigold's murder was linked to Laura's. Almost two years had passed since Laura's death, but he couldn't dismiss the possibility. And there was Crabbe lurking about, still free. How might he alert Hebe while not giving her away to her mother? If he did manage to get word to her what good would it do?

He rose and served himself eggs and bacon from the warming dishes. At the table, he glanced out of the window. No sign of rain, he would lend a hand to get that fallen fence fixed. And, as he remained longer than he'd intended, he would take pity on his annoyingly loquacious valet and send for him.

Chapter Nine

THE DAYS PASSED slowly while Hebe's mother regained her strength and vigor. On a misty afternoon which kept her aunt indoors working on her charts, Mama asked Hebe to walk with her in the garden.

"I intend to take the stage next Wednesday," Mama said as they strolled over the lawns toward the stream, the air still and moist and smelling of wet earth. "I will write to you as soon as I can after I reach your grandfather's home in Tunbridge Wells, to let you know I've arrived safely." In response to Hebe's concerned expression, Mama squeezed her arm. "Please don't worry that I'm abandoning you. I need to talk to your grandfather as I have said. He may be in financial difficulty. His grief on losing his son will have affected him deeply. It always helps to talk about these things. There might be something I can do to help. What I don't wish to happen is for you to languish here when you should at least be attending the assemblies in Brighton where you might meet a suitable husband. I shall speak to your aunt about it before I leave.

"Brighton is a popular place with the *beau monde*," Mama said. "In the summer, many visit the town to enjoy the balls the Prince of Wales holds at the Royal Pavilion. Your father and I attended one once, it was dreadfully crowded and noisy, and so hot I feared I would faint. But it is the most remarkable building, and the exotic décor so very striking. I hope that your aunt will take you there."

Hebe suspected her mother's request could fall on deaf ears, but she refrained from saying so. She worried about her going off alone on another exhausting journey. What would happen if she was turned away at the gates of Longford House? "I will miss you, Mama." She kissed her cheek.

Mama smiled sadly. "How blessed I am to have such a good daughter."

Would Mama think that if she knew the truth? That her daughter was an artist's model? Hebe couldn't deal with that now and pushed the thought away.

On the day before her mother was to depart, a letter arrived for Hebe. It was handed to her mother while Hebe was in the garden assisting her aunt with the hives.

When she came in her mother was studying Sally's handwriting with a perplexed expression. "Who is Miss Sally Fortune?"

Hebe tamped down the impulse to snatch it from her. She held out her hand. "Someone I met in London where I worked."

Her mother frowned. "It might be best if you put the dreadful episode behind you, Hebe." But she handed the letter to her without further comment. Hebe scurried upstairs to read it. It was so good of Sally to write. She hadn't expected a letter.

The vision of Sally laboring over it made Hebe smile fondly. She missed her. While sitting on the bed, it took her a few minutes to decipher the scrawled lines on the page. When the message became clear, she cried out in horror. Marigold murdered! Was it her horrible brother, Seth? She read on and discovered Marigold had been found strangled near Ashe's home. Had she gone there looking for work, perhaps at night... and...

Hebe gasped. Strangled! Oh, what a horrid way to die. A distressing vision of Marigold, so full of life swam before her eyes. She jumped up and fumbled in the drawer to take out a fresh handkerchief. Hebe was blowing her nose when her mother hurried in.

"My dear girl! I heard you cry out. What has happened to upset you?"

"A friend has died, Mama. Sally has written of it."

"Oh, how very sad. I am sorry. Was she a servant at the inn?"

Hebe shook her head and muffled her reply with her handkerchief.

"She was ill?"

"She was murdered. They don't know who did it."

"Good heavens! London is such a dangerous place. I'm glad you're safe here, Hebe."

Hebe gave a trembling sigh. "Yes, Mama."

After the door closed on her mother, Hebe lay with her head on the pillow. Surely, the awful news must have reached Lewis. He might have written to her, but of course, he couldn't because he didn't know where she was.

A horrifying thought crept unwelcome into her mind. If she hadn't taken Marigold's place posing for Lewis, would Marigold still be alive? She turned her face to the pillow.

By the end of the week, Lewis and his tenant farmer, Joe Brown, were enjoying an ale at his farm house, congratulating themselves on their handiwork as the trench filled with water from the stream. That afternoon, Dunstan arrived and began to sort through Lewis' clothes in his dressing room while still managing to convey a measure of hurt.

"I feel I must point out, milord, your clothes require a good deal of attention, and you are not turned out as well as you might be."

"I quite agree, Dunstan. I am inordinately pleased you're here to attend to them."

Much mollified, Dunstan gathered up a pile of shirts and tut-tutting, left the room.

On Saturday evening, Lewis had dutifully attended the assembly in Bath, and danced with several young ladies, including Miss Amy Banbridge, much to her mother's delight. He was promptly invited to dinner. As he could see the way the wind was blowing, he politely refused saying events had conspired to take him away for a few days.

He would drive down to Brighton. Perhaps he'd find Hebe at a social event in the town, and a means of alerting her to the possibility that Crabbe was dangerous could present itself. Especially if she meant to return to London soon.

Seth was the obvious suspect in Marigold's murder, but it seemed passing strange for a brother to kill his sister in that manner. Seth might have hit her; he obviously had a foul temper, but strangle her? A cold-blooded way to kill. It spoke of a ruthless blood lust. And why would he when Marigold was Seth's meal ticket? Even so, Hebe must be warned. Especially as she'd made her dislike of Seth plain to him. If he was the revengeful, murderous sort capable of such senseless violence, she could be in danger.

Lewis was occupied with matters requiring his attention before he left for Brighton, when Sarah came to tell him there was a lady at the door.

"Who is it?" Lewis feared it might be his neighbor's wife making a morning call.

"The lady didn't give her name, milord."

Surprised, Lewis put down his pen and pushed back from the desk. "Send the lady in, Sarah."

A moment later, in walked Lady Adela, his former mistress dressed in a fetching blue habit trimmed with lace, her black hat sporting a jaunty feather. She removed her tan York gloves, a faint smile on her face. "Lewis. How nice to see you."

Their last meeting was anything but pleasant when she threw her new lover's name at him along with an expensive vase. He raised an eyebrow. "Is it?"

"You might be more gracious and invite me to sit down; I've ridden all the way from Lord Piper's estate. He's holding a house party."

Lewis remembered his manners and bowed. "Please be seated, Adela. May I offer you tea, or wine?"

"Brandy, thank you." She untied the strings of her riding hat, lifted it from her head and sought to order her riotous blonde curls. "I rather hoped you might ride back with me. Many of Piper's guests are acquaintances of yours. An archery contest is to be held." She smiled. "You were always good at sports, as I remember."

"Some other time, perhaps."

"Are you now a recluse?" Seated on the Moroccan leather armchair, she crossed her slim ankles and surveyed him, her pretty face as beguiling as ever. "Must I suffer guilt for leaving you?"

"No, to both those questions." Lewis walked over to the decanter of brandy warming on a tray near the fire.

"Just a drop, thank you. I shouldn't like to lose my seat."

He glanced over his shoulder. "I shouldn't think it likely. You are a good horsewoman."

She still pouted at him, no doubt when some measure of praise for her very fine derriere wasn't forthcoming.

Lewis poured her three fingers of the deep, caramel-colored liquid and handed her the goblet. Ignoring it, she reached out and took his free hand in hers. "Have you missed me?"

He sighed and gently withdrew it. "I've been busy, Adela."

She narrowed her green eyes and took the proffered glass. "Who have you been busy with?"

"I don't see that it concerns you."

She tossed her head. "I haven't heard of you courting a lady, perhaps it's one of your models. You do seem to prefer the demi-monde, the last one I remember was a redhead, Marigold, wasn't that her name? Are they more fun in bed, Lewis? I can be too if you wish."

Lewis eyed her distastefully. What had he seen in Adela? The widow had come into his life during that turbulent time just before Laura died after he'd learned from a so-called friend that he was being cuckolded. Why do these do-gooders feel it's their duty to tell a fellow his wife is straying? But Lewis refused to use it as an excuse for the affair with Adela.

He'd wanted her and saw no reason why he shouldn't enjoy what she offered. However, he had quickly tired of her flying into a temper and accusing him of pursuing other women.

After Laura died, he'd had no taste for any of it, but Adela had been disinclined to leave him. Fool that he was, he'd still succumbed, because for a while, it blotted out the horror of Laura's death and his culpability.

He perched on the edge of the desk as the smooth, flavorsome brandy warmed its way down his throat. If her relationship with Piper had become intimate why come to see him?

"How is Lord Piper?"

"Attentive."

"Then why not encourage him?"

She shrugged, put down her glass and rose. With a sway of her hips, she crossed the floor to him. "I heard you'd left London, and I wanted to see you."

"There's nothing between us anymore, Adela. It finished months ago."

So close, her skirts brushed his leg and her familiar perfume flooded his senses. She smiled slightly and traced over the embroidery on his silk waistcoat. "It will never be finished between us. You know that."

When she raised her hand to touch his face, Lewis slid off the desk and circled her slender wrist with his fingers. Then he released it. "Allow me to see you out, Lady Adela."

A look of fury appeared in her green eyes and vanished just as quickly. "Perhaps you do have another lady tucked away, Lewis." She gathered up her hat and gloves and crossed to the door. "I shall be interested to learn who she is."

"If I did, I would make no secret of it. Why does it concern you? You should bring Piper up to snuff, Adela. He has deep pockets."

She turned swiftly and raised her hand to slap his face.

He caught her wrist in midair.

For a moment she glared at him. Nothing was said. The only sound in the room the clunk of the grandfather clock. Lewis dropped her hand, stepped back, and bowed.

"I'm sorry, Adela. I guess we are destined to make each other unhappy. But I do wish you well. Your groom holds your horse?"

Adela nodded, an expression in her eyes he couldn't read.

"Then I shall say good day." He opened the door and stood aside to allow her to pass across the threshold.

"Goodbye, for now, Lewis." She briskly pulled on her gloves. "I shall be kinder to you than you've been to me... when you come crawling back."

Women were more trouble than they were worth. If he'd forgotten it, Adela had just reminded him.

Through the window, he watched her settle the black beaver hat over her curls as she walked down the path to where the groom held the reins of a dainty chestnut mare. Adela wasn't just beautiful she was clever. But there was something in her nature which destroyed any chance of happiness with one man. Despite his dislike of her behavior and his, he suffered a moment of compassion for her. Fortune didn't smile on widows. Her husband's heir had inherited the estate and although she'd been left with a comfortable stipend, it wouldn't continue to support the extravagant life she led in Mayfair forever. As her finances dwindled, she would be planning her future. Piper was a widower and she might be holding out for marriage. Had she hoped to use him as a means of making Piper jealous? Her beauty was peerless, and she might bring Piper to the altar. He hoped she did.

He turned away, struck by how different Hebe was. She had every reason to rail at fate, to be as sulky and dissatisfied with life as Adela, and yet she wasn't.

These thoughts lingered as he continued to prepare for his journey south.

Chapter Ten

TWO THINGS HAPPENED to make life a little more bearable for Hebe. Her mother's letter arrived. She'd reached Tunbridge Wells safely and was now staying at Longford House. The few lines described her mother's journey, but gave no clue to her grandfather's disposition. Still, Hebe was intensely relieved that for the moment, her mother was safe. The other more surprising occurrence was her aunt's intention to attend the Brighton assembly on Saturday evening.

"It's been many years since I attended one of the dances," Aunt Prudence said sounding oddly girlish as they readied themselves for the evening's entertainment.

Mary did Hebe's hair, and although her aunt's remained in a stern chignon, Hebe's fair hair was drawn up on top of her head and coaxed into curls around her face with the use of heated tongs. The only decent dress she had to her name was a muslin sprigged with bunches of violets, a lilac ribbon sash around the high waist and frills edged in the same ribbon around the hem and short sleeves. Hebe liked wearing pretty dresses and cast a sad thought for the lovely gowns fashioned for her first Season.

Standing before her in purple crepe, still in the style of many years ago, her aunt surveyed Hebe. "Perhaps you'd like to wear one of my chemisettes. It will be warmer."

Hebe put a protective hand on the pretty bodice. "No, thank you, Aunt. I have my pelisse, and it will be warm inside the ballroom."

"I have just the thing."

Hebe grew nervous as her aunt returned to her bedchamber. But when she came back, she handed Hebe an exquisite shawl.

"It's beautiful, Aunt." Touched, Hebe looped the shawl over her elbows and gazed in the Cheval mirror. Woven in a sinuous floral pattern of blues and greens, it was so fine and light it might have floated away.

"I purchased it in India. They make better shawls than the French. The design is called paisley. You may keep it."

"Oh, but I couldn't."

"Nonsense." She peered out of the window. "Diggory has brought the carriage around. We'd best take umbrellas as it looks like rain."

Fortunately, the rain held off for the short but bumpy journey to Brighton. Passing through the narrow lanes, they were deposited on the pavement in Ship Street outside the Old Ship Inn, a white, four-story building with bow-fronted windows overlooking the sea. There was a strong briny smell in the air. Only a few yards away, waves broke against the seawall with a roar and sent up an arch of spray, crystalline in the light of the moon.

Caught for a moment by the ocean's might, they turned to pass through the white columned entrance into the crowded ballroom.

Beneath the twin chandeliers in the high arched ceiling, a quadrille was in progress, the dancers performing the intricate steps.

It had been so long since Hebe had danced! Memories rushed to greet her as she and her aunt took seats along the wall. She saw no one she recognized, but still flushed with embarrassment when recalling the frosty reception, she and her mother had received, if not the cut direct then certainly some measure of it. After the newspapers related the stark details of her father's disgrace and his death, it was discussed behind fans and in corners wherever she and her mother went.

Aunt Prudence drew her fan and a scented handkerchief from her reticule. "It's very warm tonight. A sure sign of rain. Oh," she craned her neck, "There's Mrs. Meldrum. It's ages since we've talked." She smiled at Hebe. "Will you be all right here alone for a moment if I have a few words with her? We share an interest in the Tarot."

"Of course, Aunt, please don't worry about me."

Left alone, Hebe felt as if every eye in the room was upon her. After the quadrille ended, the dancers, laughing and chatting, returned to their seats. Some glanced at her and whispered to each other. This year's crop of debutantes made Hebe feel ancient. She'd begun to wish she hadn't come. How foolish to believe she could find a way back into the *ton's* favors.

Two older ladies seated themselves next to Hebe. One of them observed her with raised eyebrows. She employed her fan and whispered to her companion. The other lady leaned forward to get a better look at Hebe. Then they both rose and walked away arm in arm, taking a turn about the room. Hebe imagined her presence would now spread through the room like wild-fire.

As a waltz was struck up, Hebe felt terribly exposed. She gathered up her fan, shawl, and reticule, having decided to wait for her aunt in an anteroom. A pair of gleaming black shoes and long, darkly clad legs appeared before her.

"May I have this waltz, Miss Fenchurch?"

Her gaze flew up to the elegant man in his evening clothes. *Lewis!* She looked into smiling brown eyes and clamped her lips to stop crying out his name. "Yes, thank you, Lord Chesterton." She put down her things, aware that as an unattended female she attracted attention.

With her gloved hand on his arm she allowed him to lead her to the dancers on the dance floor.

The music swelled and Lewis, his hand in hers and the other at her waist swung her into the dance. "How charming you look tonight, Miss Fenchurch." He lowered his voice as he led her over the floor. "I thought I'd take a chance on finding you here."

For a moment, Hebe wondered if this was a dream. "Poor, poor, Marigold," she murmured cautiously eyeing a couple dancing near them.

His hand tightened around hers. "So. You've heard."

"A friend wrote me about her. It's so dreadful, I can't quite believe it."

Lewis glanced around him. "We can't talk here. Could you meet me in the ante chamber near the entrance at eleven o'clock?"

"I'll try." Lewis was an excellent dancer, and breathing in his familiar cologne, she allowed herself to be swept away as he led her over the floor. But when the dance drew to a close, her nervousness returned.

Her aunt had returned to her seat when Lewis escorted Hebe from the floor. "I'm sorry I was so long away, Hebe." She eyed him. "Please introduce me."

"Aunt, I should like you to meet Lord Chesterton. My aunt, Lady Prudence," Hebe explained to Lewis.

Lewis bowed. "Good evening."

"You have been introduced to my niece, Lord Chesterton?"

"Indeed yes. I had the pleasure of her acquaintance in London."

Her aunt nodded. "Then you must call on us."

"Delighted." With another small but graceful bow, Lewis left them.

Aunt Prudence employed her fan. "My, he is handsome. Chesterton? Now I seem to remember..."

"I hope your conversation was informative concerning the Tarot, Aunt," Hebe said hastily. "I meant to ask you. Have you made any new discoveries concerning my astrological chart?"

"As a matter of fact, there is something interesting I meant to discuss with you. It's about Pluto..."

As Aunt Prudence launched into her indecipherable astrological language, Hebe allowed her thoughts to flow. Had Lewis learned something more concerning poor Marigold? Why would he come all this way if not to warn her? She shivered as if some dark shadow had crossed her path.

"Are you cold, Hebe? You should have worn my chemisette..." Her aunt broke off her attention caught by a gentleman crossing the floor toward them. A man of some fifty years, he bowed before them slightly restricted by a thick waist. "I do declare it's Lord Buckwood. Good evening, milord."

"Far too long, Lady Prudence. I've missed our interesting talks concerning apiary. Now, who is this lovely young woman?" His pale eyes rested on Hebe.

"My niece, sir. Miss Hebe Fenchurch," Aunt Prudence explained. "Daughter of Christopher Fenchurch the 5th Baron Forth."

Recognition flashed into Buckwood's eyes, followed by speculation. "May I join you?"

"But of course."

He threw up the tails of his coat and sat.

Aunt Prudence immediately drew Buckwood into a conversation about the importance of bees in the natural world.

Hebe didn't care for the look Buckwood gave her. She tensed with the uncomfortable realization that she had no idea what her aunt might do next. And little confidence that rakehells would be given short shrift. Her aunt's attitude toward the *ton* was ambiguous. Nor had she exhibited any real interest in Hebe's wishes or dreams, except as to how they fitted with her charts.

She smiled and nodded, while they conversed, trying not to show how uncomfortable she remained under Buckwood's hard gaze, while her mind dwelled on Lewis. She glanced at the clock. Time grew short and Buckwood seemed to have settled in for a long chat.

She must think of a means to slip away before eleven o'clock.

Buckwood cleared his throat. "Do you ride, Miss Fenchurch?"

"Oh yes. I do enjoy it, but I don't ride often, and I have no horse stabled here."

"I don't approve of those animals for hire in the Brighton stables. I keep horses here. I should be delighted to mount you on my mare. Would tomorrow be convenient?"

Horrified, she could've bitten her tongue, she should've been paying more attention. She looked to her aunt, desperate for her assistance. When Aunt Prudence failed to offer any objection, Hebe seized on the only thing she could think of. "I'm afraid I didn't bring a riding habit with me."

"We must have one made," Aunt Prudence said. "Perhaps you might ask again, Lord Buckwood. Do you stay long in Brighton?"

"I'm afraid I must return to London soon. But I shall call on you tomorrow."

His heated purposeful gaze made Hebe's stomach churn.

When he finally left, Hebe felt like a wrung-out sponge. And the clock had struck eleven. She rose to her feet. "I must go to the ladies withdrawing room, Aunt."

Aunt Prudence reached for her shawl "I shall come with you."

Hebe glanced toward the door as they crossed the busy room, their way constantly restricted by groups of chatting people.

"Prudence! Can that be you? I had no idea you'd returned to England." A gray-haired lady in gold lace hurried over to them.

"I am here as you see, Amanda. Hebe, I should like you to meet Lady Stowe. Amanda, my niece, Hebe."

Lady Stowe raised a pince-nez and stared at Hebe with one enlarged blue eye. "Your brother's child, Prudence. How sad. So very, very sad. I was away from London during that time. My daughter, Chloe was increasing. She gave birth to a fine boy which has pleased my son-in-law immensely. Please accept my belated condolences and sit with me. I wish to learn how you go on."

As their conversation seemed to exclude her, Hebe seized the moment. "I must go to the ladies' withdrawing room, Aunt," she said managing to convey a sense of urgency.

"Yes, yes, do, Hebe," her aunt said, vaguely waving her away.

Hebe didn't wait for her aunt to change her mind, she darted through the crowd.

Lewis cursed when half a dozen guests wandered into the ante room. A billiard table had been set up, and a game was soon organized. It would be impossible to speak privately here without attracting attention. It appeared that Hebe's life had taken a turn for the better, and he did not intend to endanger it. In that gown she looked every bit what she was, a gently reared and lovely young woman. Some beau would snatch her up soon enough.

He doubted Hebe would know anything new about Marigold. Although he'd like to discuss it with her, he should do the sensible thing and leave.

He glanced at his pocket watch. Ten past eleven. It appeared Hebe wasn't coming. Lewis left the ante room and made his way to the front door.

"My lord!"

Hebe came hurrying behind him. "I had trouble getting away," she gasped her cheeks pink.

Caught again by her fresh-faced innocence, he considered it extraordinary how untouched she seemed by the life she'd been living in London. If that life had continued, however, this lovely girl would have been damaged by it.

He glanced behind her, but no one had followed, so he drew her into a shadowy corner. "We shouldn't be seen here alone together, Hebe. I came down hoping to find you. To warn you to be careful when you return to London. If Seth Crabbe was behind Marigold's murder, he might be dangerous."

"Have you learned anything more?" Hebe asked. "My friend, Sally has no idea what happened although she suspects Seth. Do you believe it was him?"

"I cannot say." He shrugged. "But it is certainly possible. Is there anything you can tell me about Marigold that might help find who killed her?"

"No." She sighed. "I don't like to engage Sally in correspondence, and I won't be in the city for some time."

"What if I went to see her?"

Hebe looked doubtful.

"Perhaps not." It was unlikely someone from that world would speak freely to him. They didn't trust the upper classes. Sometimes for good reason.

"I do appreciate you coming all this way to warn me," Hebe said.

"I wanted to get out of London for a bit..." he began.

Loud voices erupted from around the corner.

His hand on her arm, Lewis pulled her farther into the shadows and shielded her with his body. "You should return to your aunt."

"I will in a minute. Is the statue finished?"

"No. I've put it aside. It's not a commissioned piece."

"Oh, but it's beautiful. You must finish it."

He smiled at her. "I lost my inspiration when I lost my model."

Hebe flushed and lowered her chin. "You must find another model. I would like to see it one day should it be exhibited in a public place."

"Yes," he said thoughtfully. "I'd like you to see it. After all, you spent many hours posing for me." He found himself wanting very much for her to see it finished. To watch her expressive face when she viewed it.

"You paid me well. Too well. I intend to return half the money when I can."

"You can forget that for I won't take it."

She shrugged her slim shoulders which drew his eye to her smooth pale bosom revealed by the gown's scooped neckline. Why had he resisted seeing her unclothed? Was it because he feared he might find her a little too attractive to resist? He considered himself a cut above those men who toyed with debutantes, and Hebe was very much one, standing there before him in her muslin gown. But without so much as a gold locket, bracelet, or brooch, he noted. She hadn't been completely restored to her former life.

Suddenly three young gentlemen burst into the corridor and ran toward them, laughing and shoving at each other. One beau knocked against Lewis's shoulder and the fellow behind him stumbled into them both. Lewis grabbed Hebe around the waist and pulled her aside before she could lose her balance.

"I say sir, I do apologize," one of the young blades said with a grin. "I didn't see the young lady."

"No harm done, but it would be better to take your hijinks outside," Lewis said, as, laughing, the young men burst out into the street.

Hebe stiffened within his arm and he turned. With a scowl on her face, Hebe's aunt approached, accompanied by the lady in gold lace.

Chapter Eleven

AT HER AUNT'S expression, a lump choked Hebe's throat. Behind her, Lady Stowe's face was a picture of pure glee.

"I ran into Lord Chesterton in the passage and while we were conversing, some rowdy young men almost knocked me off my feet," Hebe hurriedly explained.

"A likely story," Lady Stowe emerged from behind Aunt Prudence to condemn Hebe with a disbelieving stare.

"As my dear brother lies below ground, I feel it is my duty to take his role in the care of his daughter." Aunt Prudence sounded uncharacteristically firm. "If you have our address, sir. I shall expect you tomorrow at two."

Lewis bowed. "Certainly. Good evening." He walked out the door.

Shocked, Hebe stared after him. She turned to her aunt mouth agape. Would Aunt Prudence have behaved in this fashion if the annoying Lady Stowe wasn't present? Much was being made of something entirely innocent. She had explained, so surely it would come to nothing. But she wished she could be sure of it.

"I should not like to be in your shoes, Prudence," Lady Stowe said. "As I've told you, Lord Chesterton has an unsavory reputation in London. He would have to be brought up to snuff."

"That is entirely unfair," Hebe said heatedly. "His lordship is a decent man, a celebrated sculptor."

"That's enough, Hebe," Aunt Prudence said. "Fetch your things. We shall go home."

"I shall leave you to deal with this, Prudence," Lady Stowe said sounding regretful, as if she would have liked to enjoy more of it.

On the way home in the trap, Aunt Prudence broke a long silence. "As I was saying earlier, Pluto has made an appearance in your chart, Hebe. It represents those hidden things that lie below the surface." She nodded at Hebe. "It is also linked to rebirth. The symbolism is clear. It shows us a way forward. Negotiate this hurdle and a new beginning is possible."

"What hurdle, Aunt?" Hebe found it hard to speak her throat was so dry. "It can't be anything to do with Lord Chesterton, he was merely being polite. He steadied me when I almost fell."

"Tonight, everything happened for a reason," her aunt said, at her inscrutable best.

Hebe was caught between asking her aunt's meaning and the fear that the answer would be even more distressing. She swallowed and lapsed into silence. When they arrived home, she said goodnight and retired with little expectation of sleep.

In the morning, after a restless night, she dragged herself from her bed and allowed Mary to help her dress. She barely touched her breakfast, ate even less at luncheon, and by the afternoon, had developed a dreadful headache. She simply must talk to Lewis alone.

Her thoughts of Lewis promptly scattered when a carriage drew up outside and Lord Buckwood descended to stride purposefully to the door.

Buckwood entered the parlor and greeted her aunt, then turned to her, his hard eyes assessing her from head to toe. He threw up the tails of his coat and sat on the sofa. "You look delightfully fresh in the light of day, Miss Fenchurch."

Hebe lowered her gaze to her hands. "Thank you, sir."

Her aunt murmured an excuse and promptly left the room.

"I should like to see more of you." Buckwood's arrogant expression seemed to suggest he expected her to fall at his feet in gratitude.

"Of course, sir. But I have so many invitations, I'm sure I shall never manage to attend them all," Hebe said, hoping he wouldn't contradict her.

His expression heated. Unfortunately, this appeared to affect him like a moth to the candle flame. "You are popular of course. I see I shall make it my business to travel down to Brighton more often."

Hebe was weak with gratitude to see her Aunt come into the room, carrying one of her special bottles of wine.

Buckwood eyed it suspiciously, declined and rose. "I am leaving for London this afternoon. I shall call next week," he announced.

"We will look forward to it," her aunt said, showing him to the door.

"Well, it seems we have another suitor," Aunt Prudence said with a great deal of satisfaction when she returned. "That means competition."

"Aunt, I don't wish to marry either of them."

"What nonsense, Hebe. This is your opportunity. You do wish to marry? This astrological alignment may not return for years. You must take advantage of it." Her aunt hurried out again.

Hebe wondered if it might be true. Her aunt seemed so sure. She ran to the window in time to see Lewis' curricle pass Lord Buckwood's on the driveway.

Lewis leapt down as Diggory came forward to take the reins. He ran lightly up the front steps and knocked. As Mary went to answer the door, Hebe hurried to the parlor mirror to tidy her hair. Too pale, she pinched her cheeks and bit her lips.

The maid announced him and left.

Lewis stared around the parlor surprised, perhaps, by the modest furnishings, although it might be Aries, tugging at his trousers, or Bertie, perched atop a lampshade.

"Stop please, Aries," Hebe ordered. The dog returned to his basket and with a disappointed growl, turned around twice and sat. "And don't you cause trouble either, Bertie," she said to the bird whose beady eyes watched Lewis.

Hebe was pleased to have him to herself for a moment while her aunt was distracted by something taking place in the kitchen. "We must confess the reason you came was to warn me about someone we both knew. Then all will be well, Lewis." She kept an eye on the door. "After all, we've nothing to hide."

"Don't we?"

Startled she looked up into his face. "We won't mention my posing for you, of course. We have already said we met socially."

"And if Lady Stowe was to begin asking questions in London?"

"She wouldn't. Why should she?"

"She'd be delighted to uncover something in the way of juicy gossip to spread around. A leopard never changes its spots."

Hebe widened her eyes. "You know the lady?"

"I know her sort. I've had a fair amount to do with them over the years."

"As have I," Hebe said, downcast. "Please do sit down. My aunt shall be here shortly."

"We must quickly come up with a story." She sank onto the sofa while Lewis took a wing chair covered in faded brocade. "Then my aunt will understand." She wished she could be more confident of that. Aunt Prudence was obsessed with her interpretation of some astrological sign, and Hebe feared she wouldn't budge.

Lewis left his chair and came to sit beside her on the sofa. He took her hand in his, his fingers, rough to the touch, recalling the wonderful statue. "Hebe. I am not the sort to be brow-beaten into something I don't wish to do."

Hebe cleared her throat, pleased that he wasn't, but at the same time greatly distracted by his touch. "No, I can quite believe that." She tried to draw away, but he held her in a loose but determined grip. "You are decent and kind..."

"I have given this considerable thought. And although it's not a love match, I am sure we can deal well together. Marry me, Hebe."

She suddenly couldn't breathe he was too close. "What? No! You are doing this for me. I won't let you—"

"I must warn you, however, that my reputation just now isn't sterling. And you deserve so much better than me."

"Your reputation?" Hebe giggled, feeling slightly hysterical. "What about mine?"

Aunt Prudence entered the room, looking pleased. "Ah, good afternoon, Lord Chesterton. I see you two are getting along famously."

Lewis stood and bowed. "Lady Prudence."

Hebe wrung her hands. "Aunt, this has all been a dreadful mistake."

"It seems that way to you, Hebe," Aunt Prudence said sagely. "But that is because it is impossible to understand when Pluto clouds the issue."

"Pluto?" Lewis widened his eyes.

"My aunt is a devotee of astrology," Hebe explained.

"How interesting," Lewis said politely.

Hebe feared she'd begin to giggle again. Was this a dream? If she pinched herself would she wake up? But it was no dream, for Lewis repeated his offer of marriage to her aunt, while her aunt nodded thoughtfully.

"So, if Miss Hebe will accept me, we can be married here in Brighton," Lewis said calmly, sounding as if he spoke of how nice it would be to have a picnic in such fine weather.

"An excellent idea, Lord Chesterton," Aunt Prudence seized the bell and rang it soundly. "We must celebrate. I brought back an excellent vintage from my travels."

"But what about Mama?" Hebe asked faintly. "She is still in Tunbridge Wells."

Aunt Prudence looked quizzical. "She will want to attend, of course. I shall write to her immediately."

"I'll return to London and visit Doctor's Commons for the special license," Lewis said. "Perhaps I can bring your mother down with me when I return, Hebe."

Hebe jumped up. "But I haven't accepted you, Lord Chesterton."

"I'll give you two a moment alone." Aunt Prudence headed for the door. "Where has Diggory got to? The Old Ship Inn would be excellent for a wedding breakfast," she called back.

Hebe turned to Lewis in desperation. "I cannot accept you, Lord Chesterton."

He raised his brow. "Allow me to ask you properly, first, Miss Fenchurch."

As the door closed on her aunt, Hebe placed a hand on his arm. "I give you leave to go. I will explain to Lady Prudence that you have business to attend to."

A faint light appeared in Lewis' serious brown eyes. "What sort of fellow would I be absconding in that fashion?"

"A sensible one I would've thought." Hebe leaned back weakly against the cushions and folded her arms. "I know why you're doing this."

The corner of Lewis mouth lifted in a wry grin. "Good. Although I must say you've been a little slow to get the drift of it."

She frowned at him. "You are rescuing me."

He took her hand. "Has it ever occurred to you that you might be rescuing me?"

"Why? You have no need of it," she scoffed.

"We are friends are we not?" He squeezed her hand gently and released it. "A marriage of convenience will confer respectability on both of us. You, through circumstances beyond your control have had your life turned upside down. And my reputation in London has reached rock bottom. I require a wife to make me presentable. Some gentleman will sweep you up before very long. Whereas it takes time and effort for me to court a lady, and at the moment few would accept me. So I wouldn't blame you if you didn't wish to take on such a reprehensible fellow with a dark past as myself."

"Oh, please don't think it's because of that..." she eyed him, annoyed. "You are playing games with me."

He shook his head and smiled a rather sad smile. "Say you will rescue me, Hebe."

"That is probably the most unromantic proposal a lady has ever received," Hebe said, her lips quivering, half in laughter, half in distress. "But as you say this is not a love match, and I should not expect better. Very well, I will marry you, Lewis. But only so you can complete the statue."

He laughed.

As the surprising Lady Prudence returned with a dusty bottle, Lewis feared he would be required to drink, he wondered what had got into him. He'd come here to try to repair the damage caused by a misunderstanding. And then to escape without any sort of commitment. Determined not to have marriage thrust upon him, in fact. But then he saw Lord Buckwood leaving the house. A brute of a man who had a reputation for deflowering young maidens then deserting them. Rendered furious at the prospect of Buckwood getting his filthy hands on Hebe, Lewis became shocked at the way she lived. And although he rather liked the slightly odd Lady Prudence, to condemn Hebe to this life was too cruel. It spelled disaster to leave her here.

It was true, he needed a lady of good birth to improve his stocks among the *ton*. Not that he gave a damn personally, but there was Emmy to consider. He didn't love Hebe. Wasn't capable of loving a woman again. But he liked her a good deal. He admired her grit. And she would put paid to Adela and the marriage-minded mamas in search of a title for their daughters at any cost. His and Hebe's union was to be celebrated. It made perfect sense.

Most of the *ton* didn't marry for love. The few who did unerringly made each other as unhappy as he and Laura had managed to be. And yes, he could finish the statue. In fact, as soon as they were decently wed and returned to London, he would get back to work. Marigold's murder might be quickly solved, and the scandal relegated to the past. If not, Hebe was safe with him. A thought struck him. Was it that, particularly, that forced his hand? Because he'd failed to protect Laura? Whatever the reason he found the outcome pleasing.

"I have accepted Lord Chesterton, Aunt Prudence," Hebe said in a subdued voice.

"But of course," her aunt said, as Diggory entered to uncork the bottle.

Lewis' gaze slid from the butler who looked more like a bare-knuckle pugilist, to the purple wine which was splashed into the wineglasses. Perhaps this was his last day on earth, poisoned on the day of his betrothal. A smile tugged at his lips and he bravely raised the glass. "To our future!" He took a cautious sip. Surprisingly, although hardly a vintage he preferred, it wasn't bad.

An hour later, Lewis took leave of his fiancée with a modest kiss on her cheek. He removed the reins from the dark skinned giant and set off in his curricle.

He wouldn't be a man if he didn't give a thought to having Hebe naked and in his bed. After he came to terms with his regrettably lustful thoughts, he began to worry that he might make her unhappy, that she might leave him as Laura had done. This marriage had been forced upon her. He would not make love to her until she welcomed intimacy.

Dash it all, what *had* got into him? This whole business had pushed him slightly out of kilter as if he was under some sort of unearthly force. Pluto perhaps. Even so, he didn't regret it, perhaps because she was very different to the women he had known. She was unselfish and generous. And he liked the way that small dimple peeped from her cheek when she smiled. The natural way she laughed. He was very attracted to her. And with Hebe as his wife he looked forward to a future he had never expected for himself.

Chapter Twelve

LEWIS LEFT HEBE confused. One minute she was euphoric at the prospect of returning to London to reside in a nice house with him, then at the thought of them marrying, she grew nervous. He liked her she knew, but he also felt sorry for her. A widower, his wife had been horrifically murdered. Sally had told her about the awful manner in which she died. It must have broken his heart. In fact, Hebe was sure it had. How could she possibly take Lady Chesterton's place? He'd been passionately in love with his wife. But theirs would be a marriage of convenience, more of a friendship. Trouble was, she wanted a passionate marriage. Desperately. She sighed.

She understood he wished to marry again to put an end to the awful speculation concerning his past and the mystery surrounding poor Marigold. As his wife and model, she would be in the unique position to do that. But was that all he wished for? Was she to be a wife in name only? She often sensed sadness in him. And a small part of her, the motherly part, wanted to soothe him and make him better. But he didn't seem the type of man to welcome it.

And then there was the *ton*. How would they treat her? If they cut her again, it would also hurt Lewis. Could their union make it possible for her mother to return to a semblance of the life she'd once enjoyed? It pleased Hebe to think it, especially if things didn't go well with Grandfather. And whatever fears she had for herself, providing comfort for her mother made it worth the risk. *Heaven knew, she might have ended up married to Lord Buckwood. And she went ice cold when he looked at her.*

Patiently settling down to help extract the honeycomb from the beehives, Hebe listened to her aunt outline the plans for the wedding. She answered her questions as if she was oddly detached from the whole affair as if they discussed someone else's wedding. Some distant relative.

"One must have a cake," her aunt said, tapping her chin. "And of course, you'll require a wedding gown. The hotel needs to be booked, guests invited…"

Guests? Hebe swiveled to look at her. "What guests, Aunt?"

"I haven't quite decided." She rattled off the names of people Hebe hadn't met. "Your mother must be consulted, and then there's Chesterton. He will want to invite his family and friends down for the wedding."

Hebe gulped. The whole thing seemed impossible. "What about Grandfather? Will he come?"

Aunt Prudence knocked the honeycomb out onto a tray. "I imagine not. I haven't heard from him since he objected to me attending your father's funeral." She huffed out a breath. "My father was adventurous in his youth, but he does not afford women the same privilege. He believes women should marry, have children and remain in the home."

Perhaps her aunt was too much like the earl. Might that be the reason they didn't get on? But Hebe did agree with her. Women should have the same freedom as men. Although the way things were in this man's world, it was unlikely to change in the foreseeable future.

As Ladies did not attend funerals, she and her mother could not visit her father's grave. They had not been told where he was buried. Not in the family crypt in any event. Suicide banned one from a decent burial. She wanted to ask, but feared it might upset her aunt whose movements around the hives had become less orderly. Had her grandfather become cantankerous? Might Mama be facing a difficult time in Tunbridge Wells? Perhaps too awful to write to Hebe about? "I'm sorry, you and grandfather don't talk, Aunt...," Hebe began, hoping to gain some idea of the situation.

"Tosh." Her aunt waved her away with the smoking apparatus, sending the bees humming in all directions. "Tomorrow, we'll visit the jewelers in the lanes. You have nothing in the way of jewelry, Hebe. I'd like to purchase a small thing for you. Although I'm sure your husband will give you splendid jewelry."

Hebe preferred he didn't. Why should he when he'd been forced to wed her? "That's very nice of you, Aunt, but it really isn't necessary."

"Nonsense. It will be my wedding present to you."

The next day, Hebe spent the afternoon wandering the Brighton lanes with her aunt, visiting several shops. Aunt Prudence bought her a silver locket and earrings, which Hebe loved and promised to treasure always. Her aunt brushed away her thanks and walked briskly to the modiste rooms to place an order for Hebe's dress.

If Aunt Prudence was short of money—and she must be, for she sold her pots of honey at the village shop, Hebe was determined to help. She had her savings and the money Lewis had given her. The country cottage she'd dreamed of one day buying was no longer a possibility. Surprised to find she wasn't disappointed, Hebe wondered if it had been a rosy picture which would not have suited her after all.

How could she aid Aunt Prudence? Her aunt was proud and unlikely to accept any money. They entered the modiste's rooms where bolts of fabric lay upon a table with boxes of buttons, braid, and lace. Madam Chawton, was an English lady of middle years with a confident air. She suggested oyster satin and draped the fabric over Hebe's shoulder. Aunt Prudence pronounced oyster to be quite the wrong color for Hebe, which Hebe would have agreed, if she'd been able to get a word in. Her aunt then pounced on a bolt of violet blue satin stating it would match Hebe's eyes, which she thought too strong a color. Hebe wandered among the bolts of material and discovered the perfect compromise. She waited until their argument wore out, then suggested it. Thankfully, the embroidered cream silk satin to be trimmed with blond lace was accepted by them both.

Lewis used the journey to make a list. He viewed London with less of a jaundiced eye. Was there a chance that life would become peaceful and pleasant again?

He arrived at his Mayfair home too late to begin to set his plans in motion. Tomorrow, he would apply for the special license, and then visit his sister. What would Emmy make of it? Would she be pleased or dismayed? Hebe was nothing like the widow she'd picked out for him. Emmy would want to know how they had met. How much of the truth might he safely reveal to her? He didn't want to upset her. *Au contraire*, he had hopes that this marriage would ease her mind, knowing how much she worried about him. Emmy would never be condescending. She hadn't a snobbish bone in her body. In the end he was confident, that as long as Emmy didn't suspect he'd married for the wrong reasons, she'd be pleased for him.

After changing, he sat in the library with a cup of coffee reading the *Quarterly Review* and sifting through his mail.

Stubbs entered. "Sir Robert Baker is here to see you, my lord."

"Baker?" Lewis put down a letter, unnerved. He'd discussed Marigold's case with the magistrate, but he'd nothing more to tell him. Why hadn't he sent a constable with a request for Lewis to call at Bow Street?

Sir Robert was a man of some distinction, King George had created him a baronet toward the end of the last century honoring him for his creation and care of the cavalry regiment named the Richmond Rangers. Sir Robert must have better things to do than come to Mayfair to question him about his model.

Lewis moved out from behind his desk as his butler showed the gentleman in.

"Sir Robert." He walked across the room to shake his hand. "May I offer you Scottish whisky or brandy to keep out the cold?"

"Whisky, thank you, Chesterton. You've been away from London?"

"Yes, Brighton. Where I found myself a bride." He turned from the drink's tray and smiled.

"I congratulate you." Sir Robert took the tumbler from him. "Who is the lady?"

"Miss Hebe Fenchurch."

"Fenchurch?" He rubbed his brow. "Of the Kent Fenchurches? Her father became embroiled in some sort of scandal. Killed himself."

"Yes, Hebe is his daughter."

Sir Robert nodded. "I remember the case. He'd been made a scapegoat. If he'd stayed around to run the case, he had a good chance of getting off."

"Shame brings people down," Lewis said.

"Sadly that is true," Sir Robert said as he sat down.

Lewis sat on the leather armchair opposite him. "What may I do for you, Sir Robert?"

"The case of Marigold Crabbe. It could become deuced sensitive. I wondered if she might have mentioned a member of parliament while she was sitting for you."

"No. Not a word. Why?"

"Her body was found in the grounds of Holland House."

"The old rambling Elizabethan mansion off Kensington High Street? Whig headquarters."

"Yes."

"Then you don't suspect her brother, Seth Crabbe, to be behind her murder?"

"He is hardly an upright citizen, to be sure. I would prefer it to be him as it would simplify matters. Crabbe's a brute, but his sister gave him her wages. Strangulation reeks of a furious intent to kill when Crabbe might seek to teach her a lesson by taking his fists to her. We will locate him. He can't stay hidden forever."

"You are following another lead?"

Sir Robert leaned forward. "A Whig might be behind it. Which leads me to my next question. A rather delicate one, I'm afraid."

Lewis took a breath. "Yes?"

"Lady Chesterton was murdered while traveling with a member of the Whig party was she not? And he also murdered. A savage business by all accounts. And the way she was killed was similar to Miss Crabbe."

Lewis wished Sir Robert wouldn't hedge. "Laura's death was a sustained brutal attack, whereas Geoffrey Lancaster died from a knife thrust to the heart. But that's more than eighteen months ago. Nigh on two years."

Sir Robert nodded. "Quite. I shall need to look into Geoffrey Lancaster's life. The last six months before he died."

"It beggars belief that poor Marigold was mixed up with the Whigs. She was a simple girl."

"Simple girls can get mixed up with ruthless men. Especially if they are as pretty as Marigold. It is an avenue which bears investigation."

"Was she raped?" Lewis asked dreading the answer.

Ashe shook his head. "Miss Crabbe was a virgin. Her attacker may have been disturbed before..."

"What about the artist, Walter Ashe? Doesn't he live near Holland House?"

He shook his head. "The girl was found nearby, but Miss Crabbe was probably seeking work from Ashe. That morning a doctor had dressed his hand, he'd cut a tendon. Can't hold a paintbrush. I doubt he'd be able to subdue a strong young woman, let alone strangle her. I've assigned a good Runner to the case. Mr. Bright will call on you, and should you think of something in the meantime, please advise him of it through Bow Street."

"Rest assured I will. I have a vested interest in finding the answer. I expect I'll be persona non grata among the *ton* until the culprit is caught."

"Wouldn't let that worry you too much. Many are far too eager to condemn. And you have your bride to consider. I'm sorry I've had to bring this up, but necessary, as I'm sure you understand." Sir Robert finished the last of the whiskey and put down the glass. "It should be a time for celebration. I wish you both happy. Thank you for the Scotch." Sir Robert rose to his feet.

Lewis saw him out.

He returned to the fireside and sat to mull over their conversation. Could it be possible that it was not Laura the killers were after? That Lancaster had been the target? There had been a lot of speculation at the time, but the way Laura was killed clouded it. Might they now learn why she was so brutally murdered? Lewis tightened his jaw. Perhaps Marigold was randomly attacked by some fiend, some limb of Satan, who came upon her when she was alone and vulnerable.

He intended to speak to Mr. Bright and work in conjunction with the Runner. But first there was his wedding, and Hebe deserved to enjoy it, although he didn't hold out much hope that their time together would be wonderful while this dark cloud of uncertainty hovered over them. He gave himself a mental shake and sat down at his desk. He would write to Damen in Greece with the news. At least one person, apart from his family, who would be unaffected by gossip and happy for him.

Chapter Thirteen

HEBE RETURNED FROM the dressmakers to find two letters waiting for her. One was from Lewis and one from her mother. She opened her mother's letter first, eager to learn how she fared. There was nothing to concern her in the tone of the words. Apparently, her grandfather had been very ill. Mama had been called upon to nurse him. He'd rallied and spent his days in a bath chair, but was rather short-tempered.

"I have not wanted to bother him with my concerns, as I'm not sure how he would react if I tried to broach them. I was greatly relieved to receive your letter assuring me you were well and advising me of your engagement! Did you first meet the viscount at the assembly in Brighton? I can't tell you how thrilled I am for you, Hebe dear. So relieved that you will be taken care of in the manner deserving of your birthright. Is he a decent man? I believe he is to call and collect me when returning to Brighton, so I shall judge for myself! I'm afraid your grandfather is unhappy at the prospect of me leaving. I do hope he doesn't suffer a relapse. Prudence has also written giving details of the wedding. It appears your aunt has taken the matter well in hand, which surprises me, I must confess, because she always seems a rather airy-fairy sort of person. Her father has made several

withering comments concerning her, so I suspect they do not get on.

So, as you see, dearest, I am living in gracious surroundings again. I only wish you were here now, so we might talk. I have much to ask you. I am anxious to learn all about your fiancé, and where you will live after the wedding. I imagine Lord Chesterton has a nice house in a fashionable part of London. It seems fortune has decided to shine on us again. Much love, Mama.

Hebe felt a good deal better knowing her mother was comfortable and safe. And not apparently in danger of being cast out, at least before Lewis arrived to bring her to Brighton.

She turned eagerly to his letter. She did not expect his words to be like those of a lover, and they weren't. He detailed his plans for them. Directly after the wedding they were to return to London. He regretted that it was impossible at this time to honeymoon in Paris, but promised one day they would visit that city.

Hebe raised her eyes from the page. A honeymoon in Paris was for lovers. She was almost glad not to be going there.

Lewis ended the missive with his desire to see her again and how much he was looking forward to the wedding. *"You will make a very beautiful bride."* It was simply signed Lewis. Hebe read those last words over and over and decided it was his sculptor's voice speaking and not that of an enamored husband to be. Finally, she put the letter away, disappointed, although why she should be was a mystery. She knew he didn't love her.

Hebe wished she wasn't so confused about her own feelings. She should be eager to begin her new life, but she suspected she was half in love with him, and that could mean further heartbreak awaited her.

Lewis called to see his sister the afternoon before he left for Brighton. He was glad to see Emmy's brown eyes sparkle with good health, and her conversation centered on her eager preparations for their baby's arrival.

"A splendid nanny has been recommended to us. She worked in the Royal household, but is now getting on a little in years. But that only means she has developed wisdom and much experience."

"As long as she doesn't drift off to sleep while on duty," he said with a grin.

Emmy laughed and hit him on the arm. "She is not that old, goose."

"I've news of my own." Lewis sat with her on a sofa in a corner of the salon which had been segregated from the rest of the long room by a magnificent screen.

"This is new," he said examining the rustic landscape painted on it.

"A gift from Colin's parents. It is to shelter us from drafts." She giggled. "They don't want anything to happen to their grandchild or its parents."

"That's rather nice," Lewis said aware he was prevaricating. "And quite decorative."

Emmy huffed. "Your news, Lewis, have you forgotten?"

He smiled. "I am about to marry."

"Lewis! You've been very sly." Her eyes danced. "Have you been seeing Lady Sylvia Standish?"

"No, it is not that lady."

"Then who? I don't recall seeing you in any lady's company of late."

"Miss Hebe Fenchurch."

She gasped. "Hebe? I know we discussed Hebe some weeks ago. I believe she is almost as infamous as you." Emmy cocked her head, reminding him of a bright-eyed robin. "Do you love her? Or are you driven by compassion for the lady?"

Lewis folded his arms. "That's an impertinent question, Emmy, which I'm not about to answer."

Her eyes clouded. "You don't love her then. Oh, Lewis!"

"You'll like her."

"I imagine I shall. I didn't dislike her when we met during her Season. It can't be my nagging that has caused you to do this?"

He wasn't about to try to voice his concerns or his hopes on the matter. They were still far too unclear. "Now that is foolish, Emmy."

Colin walked into the room. "Are you calling my wife, foolish, Lewis?"

Emmy turned to greet him. "Colin, Lewis is to marry Hebe Fenchurch."

Colin strode over and shook Lewis' hand then dropped a kiss on his wife's cheek. "Well I say. Unlikely choice of bride perhaps, but still... that is great news. I look forward to meeting her. Congratulations! When is the wedding?"

He drew in a steadying breath. "Sunday next in Brighton."

"Brighton? Why all the way down there?" Emmy shook her head. "She isn't..."

"Emmy!" Colin frowned at her.

She sniffed. "It does happen, Colin."

"Nothing like that. Hebe's aunt lives in Brighton. She is arranging the wedding which is to be held at the Old Ship Hotel. I hope you can come?"

"I wouldn't miss it," Emmy said.

Colin shook his head. "You shall have to, my sweet. Remember what the doctor said."

"What did the doctor say?" Lewis asked with a twist of anxiety.

"It's nothing," Emmy said, her lip trembling.

"No long carriage rides," Colin said firmly.

"Oh, Lewis," Emmy put a hand to her mouth, "I hate to miss your wedding."

"I am sorry, too, Emmy. I shall bring Hebe to meet you when we return to London."

Emmy cast an anxious glance at Colin. "We wish you every happiness, Lewis. Don't we, Colin?"

"Indeed we do," Colin said.

When Lewis left, he feared his marriage might cause Emmy more anxiety than when he remained stubbornly single. Was she completely well? He had expected them to attend his wedding and perhaps should have insisted it be held in London. But better surely to hold it as far away as possible from the *ton's* gossips and return quietly to London afterward.

The next day, Lewis left London at the crack of dawn. His coach passed through the tall gates of Longford House before luncheon and drove along an avenue of aged oaks toward a rambling old house built several centuries ago. The estate, not far from Tunbridge Wells, had a fine park, the formal gardens well-tended.

A footman stood waiting at the door as the coach was driven away to the stables.

Lewis removed his hat and gloves and handed the liveried footman his card. "Lord Chesterton."

"You are expected, milord. Please come this way."

He followed the servant up the stairs. The drawing room had a low beamed ceiling and was furnished in the old style, with heavy furniture and velvet drapery. The earl sat by the fire, a shawl around his shoulders. A fusty smell lingered in the air. "Lord Chesterton, milord," the footman announced.

"Close the door, confound it, Joseph. You're causing a draft."

"Don't just stand there," he said gruffly to Lewis. "Come over here into the light."

Lewis strode across the carpet and offered the gentleman his hand. "My lord, it's good to meet you."

Longford peered up at him, his aged face creased into lines of discontent, his grip weak, his skin papery and cool. "I don't know why it should be. No one wants to visit a sick old man. I've been forgotten long before I'm dead."

Lewis wasn't sure how to reply to that.

"Well, sit down." Longford waved his cane at the armchair opposite him.

Lewis sat. He could do with a drink, but apparently wasn't about to be offered one. He trusted his coachman and groom fared better.

"So you are Chesterton," his lordship stated. Unnecessarily, Lewis thought. Was he about to have his past dredged up?

"I am, sir."

"You are to marry my granddaughter, I'm told."

"This coming Sunday."

"Good of you, considering," he said stroking his chin.

"I consider myself fortunate indeed," he said. It appeared the man didn't care tuppence about Hebe.

"I daresay. She has no dowry. I wish to make that plain."

"I have no expectation of one."

The old man nodded. "Love match then. I believe she's turned into a beauty, like her mother. Society won't accept her though, because of the scandal. But you'd know that."

Lewis wanted to leap to her defense, but feared it would make matters worse. The man was a curmudgeon.

Lewis cleared his throat. "I am to drive Lady Forth to Brighton."

"I am aware of it." The earl snorted. "But I don't have to like it. She's been looking after me. Does a fine job too. I'd discharged two nurses before she came."

So Lady Forth was now living in a better house, but as a servant to a recalcitrant old man, Lewis thought bemused. Well, he'd see about that. "Might I speak with

Lady Forth?" he asked. "We will have to leave for Brighton soon."

Longford picked up the bell on the console table beside him and rang it. When the door opened, he instructed his footman to fetch her.

Lady Forth must not have been far away, for a moment later she appeared. She was an older version of Hebe, her fair hair, and blue eyes a little faded by the years and her face marked by the anguish she'd experienced. Lewis bowed over her hand.

She gazed speculatively up at him. "It is good to meet you, Lord Chesterton. I am packed and ready. Do you wish for a bite to eat before we depart?"

"I would appreciate it, thank you. And something for my coachman and groom if you will."

She gave the order to the footman then went to a table to pour medicine for Longford. The old man opened his mouth and took it from her spoon without a murmur.

Lady Forth came to sit on the sofa. "I have many questions, my lord, but they shall have to wait until we are on our way."

"You will come back immediately after the wedding, won't you, Abigail?" Longford sounded querulous, his pale blue eyes vulnerable.

"Of course. Didn't I promise?" Hebe's mother said placidly. How like Hebe she was, Lewis thought. The same calm acceptance of her lot. Did she really want to return to this mausoleum and this cranky old man?

Longford nodded. "I shall expect you. If I am still above ground."

Abigail came to pat his hand. "Of course you will. You are getting better. I'm only sorry you cannot attend Hebe's wedding with me."

He scowled. "Weddings! Bah!"

After a strained hour spent eating chicken pie and salad and imbibing coffee in the dining room while his lordship picked at his food, Lewis said his goodbyes to the disgruntled Longford and escorted Lady Forth to his coach.

"The earl is not a happy man, is he?" he asked as the horses took off down the drive.

"No, losing his son has destroyed his peace of mind," she said. "I feel sorry for him."

"I suspect you are a paragon, Lady Forth," Lewis said with a grin.

She shook her head. "The reason I came here was to ask for his help. We have been in difficult straits since my husband died. I'm sure Hebe would have told you."

He nodded.

"But I've come to understand my husband's father a little better. He is a bitterly disappointed man."

"You don't have to live at Longford if you don't wish to. You are most certainly welcome to live with Hebe and me."

"You are very kind, my lord," she said. "But I must return here. Longford is estranged from his daughter, Prudence. I hope to see matters mended between them before he dies."

Lewis didn't comment for he rather doubted such a rift, whatever the cause, between the eccentric lady and irascible old man would be easily mended.

Lady Forth rested her gloved hands in her lap. "As we must spend some hours together, Lord Chesterton, I should like to know more about you." She smiled to soften the words, but she looked determined. Lewis groaned inwardly. What he was able to tell her, without giving away Hebe's secrets, one might write on the head of a pin.

By the time they approached Brighton, Lewis had made a small amount of information stretch to its absolute limits. While not lying precisely, he'd omitted meeting Hebe in London and anything about his sordid past. Instead, he told her mother about his sculpting, his London house, his estate, his sister, his cat, and his dogs, hoping the good lady might drop off to sleep. She remained bright eyed and inquisitive, however, asking all manner of intelligent questions. His sympathy for her, and for women who through circumstances beyond their control had found themselves in a similar position, deepened. A practical woman, he struggled to convince her that his marriage to Hebe was for all the right reasons.

The coach pulled up outside Lady Prudence's house in the early evening where candlelight brightened the windows. The door opened, and the big servant lumbered over to heft the trunk down as Hebe and Aunt Prudence appeared at the top of the steps.

Hebe hurried to hug her mother. "Are you well, Mama?"

"I am very well, my dear."

"Did you have a good journey? You are just in time for dinner," she said, finally turning to Lewis.

He placed a hand on her slim shoulder and pressed a brief kiss on her cheek. "Excellent. I am famished. And afterward I shall take myself off to the Old Ship Hotel."

Hebe took his arm with a worried glance and walked with him into the house. "I must tell you all about Aunt Prudence's wedding arrangements. She has done a splendid job sending out invitations to I don't know how many people."

His bride to be didn't appear to be happy, Lewis noted.   "I   am   eager   to   hear   it."

Chapter Fourteen

AFTER DINNER, HEBE sat with Lewis on the terrace. The night was pleasantly warm. Crickets chirped in the garden and moths fluttered around the lanterns. She felt a little like a moth herself drawn to the man beside her. "Might Lord and Lady de Lacy come to Brighton?"

"I'm afraid not. My sister is expecting a baby, and the doctor forbids long journeys."

"Oh, a baby! That is wonderful news, Lewis." She had met Lady de Lacy during her first Season in London and found her charming. "Will many of your friends and relatives attend our wedding?"

"Hebe." He took her hand, rubbing a thumb along the underside of her wrist. If he discovered the fast beat of her pulse, he didn't acknowledge it. "I wanted to invite everyone of my friends and relatives to our wedding. But in the end I decided against it."

She drew in a breath. She was relieved, but struggled with the conviction that it was her shameful past. "Because of my family?"

He frowned. "No. Because of this business with Marigold. I had a visit from the Bow Street Magistrate. The circumstances surrounding her death appear more complicated than we anticipated. It's possible the investigation could drag me into it, and by association, you."

"Goodness." She shook her head. "I'm afraid I don't understand."

"There's been a suggestion that Marigold's murder is linked in some way to Lady Chesterton's."

Hebe stared at him. In the flickering golden light of the lantern she could not make out his expression, but the timber of his voice told her how concerned he was. "They don't believe it was Crabbe?"

Lewis explained what he had learned from Sir Robert Baker.

"So nothing has changed," she said with a sigh.

"It is far better for us to return to London quietly as a married couple. I hope to keep news of our wedding from the newssheets and prevent a storm of interest settling on you."

"Oh yes, I see." And to a certain extent she did. But she couldn't help wondering if he was dismayed at the idea of marrying her and was just making a good fist of it.

He took a jewel box from his pocket and flipped it open with his thumb. A diamond ring sparkled in the light. "Lewis, it's lovely!"

He slipped the ring on her finger. "Good. It needs no alteration."

She held her hand up to the light from the lantern and sighed as it flashed like brilliant fire. She looked up wanting him to kiss her, which he promptly did. A light touch of their lips, not the passionate kiss she yearned for.

He drew her close. It seemed more of a protective gesture than desire on his part. Nevertheless, she liked to sit within the circle of his arm. She breathed in his clean male smell, finding it comforting while at the same time, unsettling.

"Who is escorting you down the aisle?"

"I don't have anyone, Lewis. I don't think Aunt Prudence would suit."

"I thought as much. I've invited a friend from my university days, Viscount Burns. Alistair has an estate not far away in East Sussex. Would you agree to have him take your father's role? He would be honored."

A strange man leading her down the aisle? She almost said no, but the prospect of walking alone seemed even more daunting. "That is good of him. I would appreciate it."

Lewis nodded. "Once this matter has been laid to rest, and the murderer has been found, we will hold a ball and invite everyone." His low voice rumbled in his chest near her ear. "At which I shall be very proud to introduce my beautiful wife."

One word sent prickles spiraling down her spine. "A ball? That would mean the *haute ton* would gather in one place and ogle her. There would be taunts and titters behind fans and a constant rehashing of her father's suicide. She could almost see and hear it.

"An excellent idea don't you agree?" Lewis said. "Everyone who meets you will understand why I married you."

Why was he marrying her? He still hadn't precisely said. She took a deep breath. This ball might be months, years away. They may never find out who killed poor Marigold. Although she prayed they would. And solve Lady Chesterton's murder too, for Lewis' sake. It seemed unlikely that the same person committed both murders.

Lewis stood and drew her to her feet. "I am very much looking forward to our wedding, sweetheart."

"Are you sure you want to go ahead with this, Lewis? I shan't hold you to it if you have given it more thought and changed your mind."

"I have not changed my mind." He gazed down at her. "Have I not made my reasons abundantly clear? I need you. And more than that, I want you for my wife."

She shook her head doubtfully.

He sighed. "Hebe." He held her close and kissed her lightly on the lips. "The marriage has been horribly rushed. We must be patient with each other. I consider myself the most fortunate of men."

Did he really? It was not what she wanted to hear, but she could think of nothing to say in response. She drew in a breath at the touch of his mouth on hers. His kisses affected her more than they apparently did him. "And I, the most fortunate of women," she said, wanting to throw her arms around his neck and tell him she loved him.

He laughed and chucked her under the chin. "Sweet Hebe. I had best depart for my lonely hotel chamber."

Early, on the morning of the wedding the weather looked threatening. Hebe glanced out of the window again an hour later and saw the clouds were scudding away. In any event, their drive to Brighton would be comfortable and dry as Lewis had promised to send his coach to collect them. She tried to swallow away the ever-present lump blocking her throat, hoping she would find her voice for her marriage vows.

"You look lovely, Hebe." Her mother adjusted the circlet of pearls in Hebe's curls. "I'm so pleased you chose this embroidered cream silk satin, and the beautiful lace. It is in perfect taste."

Hebe glanced at her mother's face in the mirror. Mama was no longer in contact with her old friends, and her family had disowned them, so there was no one she would want to invite to the ceremony. But she might have wanted to organize Hebe's wedding. When Aunt Prudence took control of the affair, should Hebe have insisted her mother was first consulted? But she hadn't been sure if it was even possible for her mother to come to Brighton. Hebe smiled at her in the glass. "It's so wonderful to have you here, Mama. Do you really have to go back to Longford?"

Her mother smoothed a piece of wayward lace on Hebe's sleeve. "Yes. I am perfectly content, Hebe. Your grandfather is ill. It's my duty to care for him. Grieving for his son and estranged from his daughter has brought him very low. And he worries about his finances although according to his business manager they are quite sound. I must confess I like being needed again." She smiled into the mirror. "You and your new husband will wish to be alone. It is only natural."

The thought sent a wave of apprehension passing through her. Her heart galloped.

"You are happy you're marrying him?" Mama asked again, sensing her change of mood.

"Of course! Isn't Lewis absolutely wonderful?" Hebe knew her burst of enthusiasm wouldn't fool her mother. "And so handsome."

"He is all that," Mama agreed, but her eyes searched Hebe's while she secured the pearl necklace at Hebe's nape. "He's a bit of a mystery though. I suspected there was much he wasn't telling me. And I wish the wedding wasn't so rushed."

Hebe wanted to tell her mother how it all came about. The way Lady Stowe had behaved and how it affected Aunt Prudence sending her on a quest to see Hebe married. She didn't. Her mother had enough to worry about. "Once we'd decided to wed we saw no reason to delay."

"No, of course not." Mama kissed her cheek. "I am thrilled for you, dearest."

Aunt Prudence entered the room with a bouquet of pale camelias for Hebe and a box containing one perfect white orchid for her mother. "These have just arrived from your intended. Her aunt wore an identical orchid pinned to the bodice of her purple gown.

"How nice of him," Mama said taking the box.

"Look inside," Aunt Prudence said.

"My! Diamond earrings!" Mama read the card. "I shall have to thank him. I see you are wearing yours, Prudence."

"Lewis is very generous." Hebe held the fragrant bouquet to her nose. "These smell heavenly."

"It's time to leave, Hebe," her aunt said briskly. "His lordship's coach has arrived."

In Brighton, the sun danced bright lights over the sea opposite the Old Ship Hotel. The small wedding party made their way to the ballroom where the vicar, the groom, and Viscount Burns a man of average height with red hair, waited. He hurried over to her.

"Miss Fenchurch," he said with a smile. "I apologize that we have not been introduced, but a groom should not see his bride before the wedding. And we do not want to risk bad luck. I am honored to have been asked to perform this special task. May I offer you my arm?"

"Thank you, Lord Burns." She rested her white gloved hand on his arm, and when the organ music began, they walked down the aisle. Hebe was conscious of the guests filling the seats. She'd met some at the assembly but couldn't recall their names. And there was the unpleasant Lady Stowe whose goading of her aunt had brought this wedding about. Hebe's glance slid away from the gray-haired lady's critical gaze to smile at her mother, Aunt Prudence, and Diggory in his Sunday best where they occupied the front seats.

Hebe raised her chin. Lewis, elegant in gray stood beside the vicar and smiled at her. She reached his side. Was that admiration in his brown eyes? She hoped it was, but she thought she saw compassion too. She didn't want to be pitied. The suspicion returned that he had acted impulsively and with noble intentions. She stood stiffly beside him as Viscount Burns stepped away.

Lewis' smile was warm and sensual. "You are every bit as beautiful as I anticipated."

This man was soon to be her husband. Despite his concerns, of which she fervently hoped she wasn't one, she knew him to be a good man. That he didn't speak of his past marriage didn't concern her. One day, they would share those painful memories, although Lewis knew more about her life than anyone, apart from Sally.

Hebe returned his smile and placed her hand in his. Was Mama right? Had fortune turned in their favor?

Lewis shouldered his way through the chatting guests to his bride's side. Hebe was bearing up well, surrounded by well-wishers, but he couldn't fail to miss the hazy expression in her blue eyes. He decided to whisk her away as soon as he was able. It appeared the guests were only casual acquaintances of hers if that. And her mother didn't know them at all. Aunt Prudence, on the other hand was enjoying herself flitting about like a purple butterfly. He didn't disapprove. She'd done her best to turn this awkward affair into something bordering on normalcy.

He sighed, glad Emmy hadn't come. She would have seen much to disturb her. His bride held herself rigid throughout the ceremony, and when he'd kissed her, her shoulders trembled beneath his hands. Would this marriage be better than the life she might have had? He wished he was sure that it wasn't for entirely selfish reasons on his part that he'd married her. Attraction, affection, and the practicality of their union didn't equate with love. And love, he couldn't offer her.

Earlier, when he'd walked with Alistair to bid farewell to him at the door, his friend had clapped him on the back. "What a fortunate fellow you are, Lewis.

Lady Chesterton is utterly charming. I would have snatched her up myself if I'd seen her first."

Lewis chuckled. "Which is why I kept her a close secret."

Alistair's green eyes grew serious. "I hope when we meet again the problems that plague you are over. I understand why you didn't wish to marry in London. But you may still face censure from Laura's relatives. Her brother might not be able to resist."

Lewis nodded. "I can handle Somerville. Michael's said and done all he can to try to wound me and failed." He frowned. "But he best take care where Hebe is concerned. As well as that friend of his Thorn."

Alistair frowned. "Thorn can be all sweetness and light if he chooses. But I hear he's a whoremonger and knocks the girls around in the Covent Garden brothels."

Lewis nodded. "Strange company for Michael Somerville. He used to choose his friends more carefully. I wonder if he knows of it."

Alistair stepped down onto the street. He turned. "See you in London."

Lewis heaved in a breath of salty sea air as he watched Alistair drive away in his curricle. Somerville wouldn't balk at spreading more vicious rumors about him in defense of his dead sibling. He was blinkered where his sister was concerned. But some of what he'd accused Lewis of in the past had enough basis in truth for him to believe it in his darkest moments.

When he made his way back inside to the ballroom, the vindictive Lady Stowe was talking to Hebe. His bride looked utterly miserable. Lewis approached them. He bowed to the gray-haired woman. "Lady Stowe."

She tittered and curtsied. "Congratulations, Lord Chesterton. I was just saying to Lady Chesterton how well the ceremony turned out, thanks to Lady Prudence. Especially when one considers the speed with which it had to be arranged."

"We are most grateful to Lady Prudence." He turned to Hebe. "We should leave soon, my love. We've a long drive ahead of us."

Hebe raised grateful eyes to his. "You must excuse me, Lady Stowe, I wish to speak to my aunt and my mother."

"I feel I must thank you, Lady Stowe," Lewis said after Hebe hurried away.

Lady Stowe simpered. "Whatever for, your lordship?"

"It was you who brought Hebe and I together."

She fingered her amethyst necklace looking pleased. "It was I?"

"Indeed. So very romantic of you."

Lady Stowe flushed. "Well, I could see you two were meant for each other."

"You are a very wise lady, Lady Stowe."

Lewis bowed and left the lady smiling.

Chapter Fifteen

HEBE SMILED AT her husband who stretched his length over the seat opposite her and her mother in the coach. He returned her smile, his eyes like warm chocolate, his coat stretched over his broad chest giving a glimpse of his fine physique. She loved him. He made her pulse gallop whenever he was near. And she liked him. She was eager to do whatever she could to make his life better. She knew it to be a daunting prospect for she feared he was still in love with his first wife. If Laura haunted his dreams and his quiet moments, what hope did she have? But she wasn't one to give up easily, and certainly not on this, which mattered more to her than anything ever had before.

He raised his eyebrows. "What are you thinking about? You look so serious and determined."

She hadn't realized she'd squared her shoulders. "Just random thoughts," she said turning to check on her mother who dozed beside her. "About what might await us in London."

"I'm rather thinking of that myself." He offered her his nonchalant lazy smile which never failed to charm her. But he could not be as at ease as he pretended. "Shall we hide away in my studio where no one can find us? I am eager to finish the sculpture."

She doubted that was possible. "Your friends will want to see you."

"I would like to introduce you to some friends, Hebe. My sister, Emmy and her husband are eager to meet you."

"Yes, I look forward to that." Hebe's throat tightened. Might it have been their disapproval of her which kept them from attending the wedding? Perhaps they thought she'd connived to catch Lewis? It did happen. Marriage minded mamas keen to have a titled husband for their daughters used all sorts of tricks. She rubbed a hand over her forehead. It was silly to worry about these things. Deal with them when and if they arose.

The coach rocked as they crossed a bridge. Around a turn in the road they approached the tall imposing gates of her grandfather's estate. "Here we are," she said, wondering what awaited them in the towering old mansion. Her grandfather had condemned her and her mother after Papa died, and nothing Mama had said led Hebe to believe he'd changed his mind. Hebe didn't understand why her mother insisted on returning and continuing to look after him. It made her wonder if her mother suffered through some sort of penance. Surely she didn't agree with Grandfather's harsh criticism?

Her mother opened her eyes. "We're here?"

"Yes, Mama."

The coach slowed in front of the house. When it halted, a footman came forward to put down the steps. Lewis leapt out to help them down. Hebe straightened her hat and faced the gloomy old house. When she was small, she suspected it to be filled with unhappy ghosts. Her mother's wish to bring the family together seemed unlikely. Aunt Prudence had shown no desire to visit her father. She preferred to remain with her beehives, her bird, and her dog, not to mention Diggory, who was her most stalwart supporter. A more attractive prospect than here where she'd suffer the condemnation of a grumpy old father who'd never approved of her.

Hebe had become fond of Aunt Prudence and would miss her. She invited her to visit them in London although she doubted her aunt would. At least, she had ventured into Brighton society again.

The paneled great hall with its beamed ceiling was hung with the heads of stags and wild boar and oil paintings which had darkened so badly with age, it was impossible to decipher their subjects. A footman informed them his lordship was resting and would join them for dinner.

A maid led them up the twisting cedar staircase to their bedchambers. Hebe wondered if Lewis would share hers, after all, it was their wedding night. But he didn't demur when allotted a separate chamber. Swallowing hurt and disappointment, Hebe wondered if Lewis considered this the wrong place for them to begin their married life. Her mother's chamber was next door with an interconnecting door. Or would he come to her in the night?

She changed into an evening gown of pink crepe then knocked on her mother's door. When no one replied, she pulled on the latch. The room was empty. As she turned away, Lewis appeared from his bedchamber. "May I escort you downstairs, Lady Chesterton?"

"Oh," she laughed. "I'd forgotten for a moment."

He smiled. "Have you ever investigated this old house? There should be some interesting family portraits in the gallery."

Her chest tightened. "Grandfather wrote that he'd placed my father's portrait in the attic. Papa isn't buried in the family plot either."

He squeezed her arm. "I am sorry, Hebe. That should have occurred to me."

Her grandfather awaited them on the sofa in the drawing room where her mother fussed with the pillows at his back.

"Good evening, Grandfather," Hebe came forward to kiss his bristly cheek. He smelled of snuff. "You have met Lord Chesterton."

His tired eyes assessed her. "You've grown into an attractive young woman," he said, managing to ignore Lewis entirely.

His flattering remark surprised her. "Thank you, Grandfather."

"No need to thank me. It was your mother's doing. Got your good bone structure from her, not the Fenchurches. Rawboned lot." Hebe's mouth almost dropped open at the fond glance he cast her mother.

"Good to see you again, Lord Fenchurch," Lewis said leaning over to shake his hand.

The old man complied while he eyed him. "Make sure you take good care of my granddaughter, Chesterton. Or I'll cut you out of m' will."

A smile toyed at Lewis's lips. "I have every intention of it, sir."

They ate at the long table in the gloomy dining room filled with heavy walnut furniture. Her mother spoke to a maid. Soon more candles were brought.

"Keen on wasting my money on beeswax, Catherine?" Lord Fenchurch asked. He sounded gruff, but Hebe could see he didn't mean it.

Her mother smiled, entirely unruffled. "Please bring his lordship's elixir," she said to the footman.

"Must I have that appalling concoction?" Her grandfather demanded. "Want to enjoy a glass of wine."

"You may have both," her mother said, as if talking to a child.

After the medicine was swallowed, her grandfather called for champagne. "We shall toast your wedding."

The courses were brought, and the covers removed releasing a fragrant steam. Hebe was hungry, she'd eaten nothing at the wedding breakfast. The dishes were unexciting but well cooked: a boiled haunch of venison, lamb cutlets, braised celery and asparagus were followed by preserved peaches in cream, and finally, a selection of nuts with coffee.

Lewis kept up a lively conversation with her grandfather drawing him out to discuss his early years spent hunting in Africa. When she and her mother left them to their port, they were chuckling together about a story involving a hyena.

She sat with her mother in the drawing room. "Grandfather seems cheerier than I remember."

"He is feeling better," Mama said.

"Due to your tender care," Hebe observed.

"He was lonely."

"Well, of course he was. He alienated everyone. Even his own daughter," she said forcefully. The fact that her mother planned to remain here to care for him still gnawed at her.

Mama nodded placidly. "I plan to have a family party here at Christmas. Prudence has promised to attend."

"She did?"

"Yes. I hope to keep your grandfather in good health until the rift can be mended."

"If anyone can, it is you, Mama."

"One can only do so much, my dear. He is an old man." Her mother poured the coffee which had been brought in by a footman. As she handed her the gold-rimmed cup and saucer, she glanced at her. "Are you happy, Hebe?"

"Yes, of course, Mama."

"You care for your new husband?"

"Yes, I do." Hebe couldn't say the words. Lewis must first hear a declaration of love from her lips.

Mama sighed. "Then God has been good."

After they retired, Hebe donned her prettiest nightgown and left her hair loose. She lay in bed wondering if Lewis would come to her. He and her grandfather were playing cards when she and her mother said goodnight.

Hebe opened her eyes to the morning light shining through a gap in the curtains. She'd been so dreadfully tired after the wedding and the trip to Tunbridge Wells that she'd fallen asleep within minutes. She sat up in bed with a gasp of dismay. Now she would never know if Lewis had come and found her asleep. And she was too embarrassed to ask him.

Once their goodbyes had been said, Lewis helped his bride into the coach and they set off for London. A fetching bonnet lined with white satin and trimmed with luscious roses framed her pretty face. She looked well rested. He had peeked in on her before he retired, perhaps with the hope that she might be waiting and invite him inside. He'd found her deeply asleep, her long hair spread over the pillow. He almost chuckled at the irony. She'd been exhausted, so it was better to leave any intimacy between them until they were relaxed and easy with each other. And alone.

He studied her curves beneath the fawn pelisse. They were alone now. He leaned forward. But despite smiling brightly at him, her eyes looked strained. "Are you worried about leaving your mother?"

"I confess I was. But not any longer. I'm convinced it's what she wants to do."

"Your grandfather is lucky to have her."

"Yes, he is. He must realize that his cruel criticism of her was wrong. Mama always cared deeply for my father. For a while after he died, she suffered dreadfully. I feared she wasn't herself."

Lewis considered how difficult that must have been for Hebe. "Does she know about your work with artists?"

Hebe's eyes grew owlish. "No. And she must never know, Lewis. It would hurt her terribly. I told her I worked at an inn."

"Your mother won't hear it from me." He didn't like to say that these things had a way of sneaking into the light of day. Artists weren't known for their discretion. Personally, he rather liked the idea of having a wife who graced artists' canvasses, but he wasn't about to say it.

"I never modelled entirely nude," Hebe said, as if guessing his thoughts. "Although I refused several offers."

"Would you have stripped for me?" he asked while trying not to study her form and allow his imagination to take flight.

"I would have done it, had you asked me to."

"Why me?"

"Because I trusted you."

Her words moved him more than he thought possible. Laura had accused him unjustly as had Adela although he'd never been unfaithful with his models. He would always cherish Hebe's trust in him. Right at this moment, he seemed to need it as much as breathing.

"Are you eager to return to work?" Hebe asked.

"Very much so." It meant sculpting Aphrodite's body, and the body which would inspire him would be Hebe's. "What do you want from this marriage, Hebe?"

Her forehead wrinkled. "Contentment, I suppose. For myself and for you, Lewis."

She didn't love him, didn't aspire to that emotion, it seemed. More disappointed than he would have believed a month ago, he cleared his throat. "I am hopeful that this marriage will serve us both. I want you to know that I shall not ask anything of you that you don't wish to give."

Hebe dropped her gaze to her hands. "Thank you, Lewis."

They fell silent as the coach continued along the road   to   London.

Chapter Sixteen

LEWIS APPEARED UNAWARE of her discomfort at having first met the butler when she applied for a position as a model. While not bending from his stiff butler stance to welcome her with any sign of warmth, Stubbs was not impolite. He had gathered the upper servants together to meet their new mistress. Lewis and Hebe then went down to the servant's hall where she was introduced to Cook and the rest of the staff.

She'd only glimpsed the receptions rooms that first day. Lewis took her through the elegant lofty rooms furnished with antiques and exotic carpets, the windows festooned with rich fabrics. On the floor above, the suite the former viscountess had occupied was now to be hers with an interconnecting door leading to a shared sitting room and Lewis' rooms beyond. She stared at the white and gilt door for a long moment, wondering if he would ever appear through it avidly seeking her company. Left alone to change from her carriage gown, she took in the subdued cream and lavender furnishings. Elegant, but not to her taste. It was important for her to put her stamp on this house. She walked into the dressing room and removed her hat before the mirror. And it was in these rooms that she would begin to make changes.

As Hebe pulled off her gloves, she looked out the window at the tree-lined street below. Then she wandered about taking a silent inventory with an eye to new fabrics and wallpapers. An excellent flower painting done by a renowned artist, hung above the fireplace. But the work was far too small for the position, and failed to hide the faded square on the silk wallpaper from where another, larger painting used to hang. Might the other painting have been a portrait of Laura? Or was she becoming too sensitive? She became aware that she was searching for some sign of the former inhabitant of these rooms because she needed to understand her and why she'd left this elegant home and her handsome husband. Laura's behavior seemed frightfully reckless and unjustified from what Hebe knew of Lewis's character. But there was nothing here apart from a few books and a lingering delicate perfume which floated out when she opened the clothes press doors.

When the maid brought hot water, Hebe washed, changed into a loose-fitting spotted muslin morning gown, and tidied her hair. She ascended the staircase where statues nestled in niches. One was of a beautiful woman. Could that be Laura? Lewis had said Laura posed for him. Was she foolish to believe she could replace this woman in his heart?

Hebe entered the library, where he had said he would be, and saw him seated at an elegant rosewood desk, sifting through his mail. He rose with a smile. "Shall I send for tea? Or do you care for Madeira?"

"Tea, please." She sat on a comfortable leather chair.

He pulled the bell cord then returned to pick up a letter from the desk. "The Bow Street Runner investigating Marigold's death has sent news."

She sat forward. "Oh? What does he say?"

"A witness has been found. Apparently, Marigold's brother, Seth was seen lurking outside Walter Ashe's home in Holland Park on the day she died."

"Then Seth has been arrested?" Expectation that Marigold's murder might have been solved made her heart beat in her throat.

Lewis scanned the missive. "No, unfortunately. He is still at large. Mr. Bright is on his trail."

Meanwhile Seth was free to do more harm. Hebe shivered.

Lewis came to perch on the arm of her chair. He reached down and placed a reassuring hand on her shoulder. "You are safe here with me, Hebe. I won't let anyone hurt you."

"I know, Lewis. I'm very grateful."

He sat on the chair opposite her. "No need for that."

A knock on the door made them both start. A footman brought in the tea tray.

When the servant left, Hebe poured the tea. She handed Lewis a cup and saucer. He took it and nodded, but seemed preoccupied. Was it because of Seth or something she said? Gratitude failed to convey how much she cared for him, yet she seemed incapable of saying more, fearing it would embarrass both of them. "When will you begin work?"

"Tomorrow." He stirred his tea.

Nervous expectation settled in her stomach.

He finished his tea and returned to his desk choosing another note. "We have a dinner engagement tonight, I hope you won't be too tired."

She swallowed. "No... of course not."

He looked up and smiled. "My sister and her husband have invited a few friends to meet you."

"Friends?" she asked in a strained voice.

"Emmy will choose wisely," he said with a smile "She tells me you've met."

"Yes, during my Season. She was most kind and agreeable. Not every lady is so generous to the fresh crop of debutantes."

She fought not to show her panic as her mind wandered through her sorry lot of clothing in search of an evening gown. Anything glamorous had been sold. She would have to alter her wedding dress and hope that Lewis wouldn't recognize it.

Lewis lifted his head from his pile of papers. "If you'll excuse me for a few hours, when I'm finished here I'll go up to my studio and make preparations for tomorrow."

She put down her cup and rose. "I'll see to the unpacking."

"Stubbs is presently interviewing young women for a suitable ladies' maid. He's sent a servant to assist you in the interim. You'll get final say, of course."

"Thank you, Lewis." Grateful that he'd considered her feelings on this matter at least, she left him to his mail.

In her chamber, the maid was shaking out her forlorn array of dresses. She curtsied. "I'm Molly, milady."

"I am pleased to meet you, Molly. Could you fetch me scissors, needle and thread?"

"Yes, milady." Molly hurried from the room.

She returned shortly afterward with a cane sewing basket. "This belongs to the housekeeper, milady."

"I have yet to meet the housekeeper. What is her name?"

"Mrs. Priddy. She is in the country at his lordship's estate at present."

Mrs. Priddy's basket was a surprising Aladdin's cave of jewel-like ribbons and bits of lace. "My goodness. We shall find everything we need here. Take out the cream silk, Molly. I wish to alter it."

Molly emerged from the trunk with Hebe's beautiful wedding gown held in her arms. "I'm told I'm good with a needle, milady."

"Are you, indeed! Then shall we begin? Some of this pale pink ribbon and the silk roses should add the perfect touch, I believe."

The freckle-faced maid grinned. "That will be very pretty, milady. And perhaps some of the roses for your hair?"

Hebe took a deep relieved breath. "An excellent suggestion, Molly."

Lewis made his way up to his attic studio. He and Hebe had been easier with each other before they married. Now a crippling politeness had descended between them. He was dammed if he understood the reason. Or how he might change it. Not by forcing his way into her bed uninvited. They would need to share some intimacy before that happened, and he admitted he was at fault. He entered the sun-filled room. A lesson in patience, for him perhaps. But he wasn't a particularly patient man.

The women he'd known were always confident of their feminine wiles. They could wrap a man around their little finger and didn't hesitate to do so when the need took them. He was certain that Hebe would never have behaved in such a fashion. Not even before her life was ripped apart.

Hebe was the most unaffected female, apart from Emmy, that he'd encountered. It was one of her qualities which he most admired. He'd come to realize that since Laura, he'd used his cynicism as a shield to protect his heart. Hebe's unaffected honesty seemed to have stripped him bare. His low moods had vanished since she entered his life. It was a double-edged sword, Lewis feared if he were swept into an imbroglio again he had nothing left with which to fight.

A bird flew above the studio's glass ceiling, its shadow darting across the floor. The room smelled of ash, candle smoke and beeswax. When he removed the cotton cloth from the statue, the sunlight fell upon the beautiful stone head and swan-like neck. Lewis ran his hands over the marble. Encountering some dimples he went to the table to select a file. He was still working when his butler appeared to advise him it was time to dress for dinner.

An hour later, as he waited in the entry hall, Hebe descended the staircase dressed in a cream gown adorned with pink ribbons and roses. More roses were tucked into her fair curls. With an urgent wish to kick himself, Lewis came forward to greet her. "What a

pretty gown and how very lovely you look in it, Hebe."
He settled the evening cloak over her shoulders. "I
imagine you will require a ballgown, and a riding habit.
I'm sure my sister will recommend a dressmaker
should you need one."

She smiled. "How generous you are Lewis."

Lewis resisted clenching his jaw as he escorted her
out to the waiting carriage. So, he was generous to a
fault, and she was grateful. Courtesy and respect had
their place, but what he wanted right now was to take
her back up to his bedchamber and remove that
charming dress, which he suspected was her altered
wedding gown. Of course she had no suitable evening
gowns, having been absent from Society for some time.
Couldn't she have told him? He was a man after all.
And most men were scatter witted when it came to
women's fashion. No, it was like Hebe to attend to the
matter herself. He smiled, determined to rectify the
situation, and see her clothed as she should be in the
finest gowns. "I am very much looking forward to this
evening."

Hebe's blue eyes clouded. "So am I, Lewis."

He squeezed her arm before he helped her into the
town coach. "I know you will enjoy yourself tonight."
He would make sure of it.

In his sister, and brother-in-law's smoky, warm
drawing room scented with flowers in vases placed on
almost every surface, a small group were chatting and
drinking wine. They all paused as he and Hebe entered.
His hand on Hebe's arm, he felt her falter, and gently
pushed her forward. Colin had chosen the guests well.
Lewis knew and liked everyone present.

"Chesterton, how long has it been?" Lord Braithwaite called, crossing the room to them.

"Too long. I have missed your ribald sense of humor," Lewis said. "Hebe, may I introduce this reprobate friend of mine to you, Lord Braithwaite?"

Hebe curtsied prettily.

"Lady Chesterton." Lord Braithwaite raised her hand to his lips. "You shall not keep this delightful young lady from us, Lewis. Invitations will be flooding in now it's known you are back in London."

As Emmy took Hebe around the room and introduced her to the guests, Lewis had no doubt that everyone here tonight would accept her.

The evening passed pleasantly with an excellent dinner, interesting conversation and afterward, whist and backgammon played at the tables set up in the salon. Lewis observed Hebe for any sign that she might be out of her depth, but because their friends would never mention her past, she seemed to be enjoying herself. After all, this was the life she had known. The one she was brought up to take her place in. It warmed him to know that he had been able to restore her to that position and tried not to think that their life spent behind closed doors may not be quite what he hoped for. He watched as she laughed at one of Lord Braithwaite's jests. She had charmed him.

Proud of her, his gaze took in the delightful curve of her cheek, the milk-pale skin of her décolletage, her abundant fair hair dressed with flowers. She was like a flower herself, and he decided that when they returned home, in good spirits after a pleasant evening, would be the perfect time to consummate the marriage.

As couples began to depart, Emmy appeared at his elbow. "Hebe has coped well."

"Yes. Thank you for doing this, Emmy."

"This was easy." She gazed up at him her brown eyes troubled. "It may not be so when you venture out into Society. There are those gunning for you who will dredge up Hebe's past."

"I know."

"You and Hebe will have to be strong and united," she stressed.

He raised an eyebrow in response to her perspicacity. "You believe we aren't?"

"I sense a restraint between you which I hope will resolve itself quickly."

"This is our honeymoon, Emmy. It takes a while to adjust."

Emmy wouldn't understand that. She and Colin had been mad for each other from the first. "The gossip is still rife concerning your model's death. It seems to have stirred up Laura's murder as well."

He moved his shoulders in a shrug of anger. "I guessed as much. Perhaps I should take Hebe to the country for a while."

"That might be wise."

"But it only puts off the inevitable, doesn't it," he said with a heavy sigh. "Especially if the murderer isn't found."

Emmy nodded. "One hopes he will be, and soon."

Colin joined them. "Lord Braithwaite is about to leave, best we see him to the door." He took her arm. "How are you my dear? Not too tired?"

"No, I am perfectly well, my love," Emmy replied. "Please do not fuss. Women have babies all the time."

"Hebe and I will say our goodbyes to everyone and depart," Lewis said. Now that he'd decided to join Hebe in her bed, he found himself suddenly impatient.

The anxiety did not fade from Colin's face as he led Emmy away. He was a serious man who tended to worry, but his concern for Emmy left Lewis uneasy.

In the carriage Lewis put his arm around Hebe and drew her close. "You enjoyed this evening?"

"I did. Everyone was so kind."

He tightened his arm enjoying her curvaceous body leaning against him. "I hoped you would." He lowered his face to her hair and breathed in fragrant lavender. "I was proud of you, knowing how difficult it is for you to face Society again. But I'm not at all surprised you did so well."

She turned her face up to him. "Thank..."

"I don't want your thanks, Hebe, or your gratitude. I am a lucky man to have married you." He lowered his head to kiss her. Her lips were soft, her breath sweet, and she placed a hand on his shoulder and kissed him back before the carriage jerked to a stop.

"I will try very hard not to thank you, Lewis," she said with a grin and the groom opened the door.

Chapter Seventeen

HEBE ENTERED THE house with Lewis. She was happy. A little light-headed from the wine and champagne, but quite definitely happy. She had feared the evening would be a disaster. But it had been delightful. Everyone so welcoming. And Lady De Lacy was so kindhearted. Hebe found no sign of disappointment or criticism in her warm gaze, and her husband was utterly charming.

As they were preparing to leave, Lady de Lacy had offered to assist Hebe with her new wardrobe. They arranged to visit a modiste she'd recommended the next afternoon. Hebe was cautiously confident that she and Emmeline would become good friends.

And Lewis kissed her. A different kiss to the light touch of lips she'd received from him in the past. This kiss spelled intent and might have deepened had they not arrived home at that precise moment. Would he visit her tonight? When Lewis inquired if she was tired after her long day she'd been careful to deny it.

On the stairs, she averted her eyes from the bust which must be of Laura, for no other model could possibly be as delicate of feature, or carved by Lewis in such loving detail, and resolutely continued to her bedchamber. Lewis had raised the suggestion of spending time at his estate. She'd visited Bath many times as a child, and the countryside surrounding that town was very familiar to her. Her memories were not all sad ones. She had enjoyed her childhood.

Molly waited for her, drooping sleepily in a chair. She jumped up when Hebe came in.

"I told you to go to bed, Molly," Hebe scolded.

"I'll sleep better knowing I've done me job proper, milady."

Hebe smiled. "Take out the white lawn nightgown with blue ribbons threaded through the lace."

"Yes, milady."

After Hebe washed and changed, Molly drew the brush over Hebe's long locks. "You enjoyed your evening, milady?"

Hebe yawned behind a hand. Heavens, she must not fall asleep in case... "Yes it was most pleasant, thank you. Don't braid my hair, Molly. And I shan't wear a cap."

In the mirror, Molly stifled a grin. She replaced the brush on the dressing table and bobbed. "Will that be all, milady?"

"Yes. Do go to bed," Hebe said amused. "I'll sleep until late morning, so don't bring my coffee until I summon you." Perhaps Lewis would be with her and they would breakfast together.

Her stomach knotting with nerves, Hebe wandered from her bedchamber to the dressing room, listening for him, her heart beating unnaturally fast. If he did choose to visit her, he should find her tucked up in bed, she decided. But she feared she would fall asleep again as it was quite late. With the amount of wine she'd drunk during the evening she wasn't sure she'd be able to keep her eyes open once her head hit the pillow. She selected one of Laura's books then climbed into bed and settled beneath the covers.

She opened the compendium of poems; a weighty tome. Did she imagine the pages smelled of Laura's perfume? Unsettled, she flicked through searching for a favorite poem of hers. A piece of paper dropped onto the coverlet. A letter, the words cramped, with some underscored. Hebe picked it up and held it close to the candle, her veins turning to ice with every word. It was direct and brutal:

Laura,

Your threat to tell your husband about us has made me angry. And you really don't want to do that. You will tell no one, Laura. Why? Because I will kill you if you do. If Chesterton or anyone learns what occurred between us, or the fellow you've discarded me for like a piece of lint on your sleeve, those you care about will die with you.

It was signed *W* with a wild flourish.

Hebe threw back the covers, bunched up her nightgown and ran across the room in her bare feet. She pulled open the door to the adjoining sitting room and stumbled into the dark. Unable to find her way forward and too panicked to return for the candle, she yelled for Lewis.

Lewis appeared through the door of his suite throwing a shaft of candlelight across the room. The silk dressing gown swirling about him his long strides brought him quickly to her side. "What has happened, Hebe? Did you have a nightmare?"

She wordlessly handed him the letter.

He took it from her, grasped her hand, and drew her back to her bedchamber. He sat with her on the bed while he read the letter.

"It fell out of a book I found in the boudoir." She watched as his jaw tightened. He cursed softly. For a moment he looked as if he didn't see her. His tight expression began to unnerve her. "Who is this W person, Lewis?"

His lips thinned. "No idea, Hebe. But I intend to find out."

She breathed in shuddering gasps and clasped her hands together, desperately sad for him and longing to ease his suffering. But she daren't touch him as he sat rigidly beside her. He was grief-stricken, and she was afraid he would brush her away. "What will you do?"

"I'll take this to Laura's brother, Lord Somerville. He may recognize the handwriting."

"Crabbe isn't the murderer?"

"Seems not."

"Will you visit Lord Somerville in the morning?"

"This must be dealt with now. It's late but he will see me." He put his arm around her and hugged her. "Are you all right?"

"Yes." She took a deep breath of his familiar scent and citrus soap.

"There are only a few hours until dawn and you need your sleep. Call your maid. She can stay with you."

"There's no need to disturb Molly," Hebe said, climbing beneath the covers. "I am perfectly safe here." She wished Lewis would stay with her, but he was already on his feet his expression one of intense resolve.

He smoothed her bedclothes. "Don't worry, Hebe. It will be dealt with."

"But whoever he is, he sounds very dangerous."

"I've no doubt he is," he murmured in a low growl.

He bent and kissed her lingeringly on the lips. "Try to get some rest. I'll see you in the morning."

Lewis strode from the room. Had he known any of this? He seemed terribly shocked by it. The writer of the letter must have feared Laura would tell, so he murdered her. Did Lewis have any idea who he was? Would he go after the man? She wasn't confident that Lewis would leave it to Bow Street to deal with him. As the door closed behind him, she shivered and pulled the covers up to her chin.

Lewis walked up to the front door of the Portland stone mansion and rang Somerville's bell. Michael might know who wrote the letter. Could Michael have kept some information about Laura's death from him? If so, it seemed unnecessarily cruel, and he struggled to believe it, even though Michael was now a bitter adversary who thought the worst of him.

The night porter opened the door.

"Lord Chesterton. Is your master abed?"

Lewis didn't feel the need to introduce himself. The porter knew him. In the past he and Michael had often played a game of chess or imbibed whiskey in his library into the early hours, and then later, after Lewis and Laura married, they'd attended dinner parties and soiree's here.

Nevertheless, the late hour, or Lewis' grave expression, gave the porter pause. After a moment, he opened the door wider and Lewis entered the vast marble checkerboard entry hall where candlelight from the wall sconces cast shadows. "His lordship has just this minute arrived home, Lord Chesterton. You will find him in the library."

"I'll announce myself." Lewis strode in that direction before the porter could react.

In the library, Michael lounged with a book on the burgundy leather sofa, a patterned silk banyan over his trousers. Walking in, Lewis felt a swift surge of sadness for the close friendship they'd once shared. All the warmth turned to cold ashes, and the man he'd once rode with, trolled the fleshpots of London with as a youth, and considered a brother, looked at him with dislike and suspicion as he rose quickly to his feet. "What the devil..."

"Don't blame the porter. I pushed ahead of him. This can't wait, Michael."

Michael raised his eyebrows and motioned to a chair. "I can't imagine what it is that won't wait until tomorrow. But please be seated. Whiskey?"

"No, thank you." Lewis took the letter from his coat pocket. He unfolded it and held it out.

While his questioning gaze remained on Lewis, Michael took it. As he began to read a vein popped out on his neck. "Bloody hell!" He raised his head and his face twisted. "Where did you find this?"

"My wife discovered it hidden in one of Laura's books."

Michael rose and went to the drinks tray. He poured out a liberal glass of whiskey. "Are you sure you don't want one?"

Lewis shook his head. He could certainly do with one, but he'd imbibed enough that evening, and he needed to keep his mind sharp for whatever came next. "Do you recognize the writing?"

"Can't say I do."

Lewis cocked a brow. "You knew more about Laura's friends than I. You have no idea who it might be?"

Michael shook his head. "I'm not about to make wild suggestions or condemn a man out of hand. Leave the letter with me."

Lewis huffed out a mirthless laugh. "Oh no. That letter goes home with me."

Frowning, Michael handed it back. He took a large swallow of liquor and his pale face flooded with heat. "I swear I had no idea that Laura was involved with anyone. She was very distressed when she came to stay here. Said you were sleeping with your models."

"Ah. So that is why you've believed the gossip and have been so damned obnoxious. I have *never* slept with *any* of my models. Before I married Laura, during the marriage, or afterward. Sir Robert Baker told me Marigold was a virgin. View the autopsy if you doubt me."

"Bloody hell," Michael said again, but with less vigor.

"You don't suspect your sister might have lied to gain your support?"

Michael stared gloomily into the golden dregs in his glass. "Laura was always wild and unpredictable. You knew that when you married her."

"She was exciting, clever, restless, and oh, so very desirable. I adored her. She broke my heart." Like a beautiful butterfly that flew just out of reach, Lewis thought. "She didn't deserve to die," he said sharply. "I have to find out who was behind it, Michael. If you have any idea, you must tell me."

Michael raked his fingers through his dark hair. "Give me time, Lewis."

"I won't give you long. You must understand why I cannot."

"Yes. Your name has been maligned, and for my role in that I am deeply sorry."

"Sorry doesn't cut it. I want the murderer."

Michael put down his glass and scraped his hands over his face. "If and when I learn who the man is, you shall have his name." He paused. "But Lewis, let the magistrate then deal with him. You can't afford to get involved in this."

"Involved? I have been for years. My life has been poisoned by it," Lewis growled. "My name dragged down in the House and every respectable drawing room in Town."

"Yes. That was reprehensible of me. I shall put it to rights as soon as I am able."

Lewis doubted it would ever be put to rights. Not entirely. Where there was smoke the public were always eager to believe there'd been a fire. He tucked the letter into his coat pocket and stood. "Twenty-four hours, Michael." He patted his pocket. "Then I must take this to Bow Street and let them find the man."

"No sense in going off half-cocked. Give me time to make some inquiries. It should be dealt with discreetly."

Had anything to do with Laura's death ever been handled with discretion?

"Marigold Crabbe's body was discovered in the grounds of Holland House, Michael. That's Whig territory. Question your friends."

Lewis left the library. When he gained the street, he slowed as he walked the few blocks to his house. The next twenty-four hours he'd allotted Michael to come up with a possible suspect, would be hell. He found it hard to believe that Michael was completely unaware of Laura's flirtations. Was he protecting someone? The sky lightened to a muted gray, and servants were stirring in the houses along the way. He passed a fresh-faced milkmaid leading a cow, and a cart rattled by. Might this new day bring an end to the nightmare he'd been living for the past two years? Michael was right; Lewis could not be the cause of this man's death, much as he'd like to be. He coiled his hands into fists. He might bring him to the brink of it, however.

Lewis reached his house and stared up at Hebe's bedchamber window. She must be asleep. His plans for how this evening would end had come to naught. Their marriage had begun so disastrously, it was hard to imagine where it might lead from here. On her first day in London, she'd been subjected to the sordid aspects of his marriage to Laura and knew the murderer still roamed free. Hebe deserved to have this matter settled. She had married a damaged man, who could offer her little beyond the basic creature comforts and a relationship which lacked true intimacy. Lewis drew in a breath as he faced the truth. He needed the tenderness of a woman's love. Hebe's love. When all this ended, if it ever did, dare he hope his life might change for the better?

Chapter Eighteen

HEBE WOKE TO the sun streaming in through the gap in the curtains. Her mantel clock showed eleven. After hours of lying rigid in bed, she had finally dropped into an exhausted sleep. Had Lewis returned to the house?

She left the bed, donned her slippers, tied the belt of her dressing gown, and rang for Molly. Ten minutes later, her maid entered with a footman who carried a tray laden with coffee pot, cream, and sugar, two cups with saucers and a plate of pastries. When the footman departed, Molly cast a sly glance at the bed. "Did you sleep well, my lady?"

"Quite well, thank you, Molly." The maid had obviously expected Lewis to be with her. Hebe didn't wish her to know she'd spent another night alone. She pushed her hair back from her face with both hands. "I shall require a bath. Oh, and I'm meeting Lady De Lacy at three. We are to visit a modiste." With all that had happened she'd almost forgotten about it. "I believe his lordship has gone down to breakfast. Have you seen him?"

"No, my lady. His valet entered his lordship's apartments as I came up the stairs."

Hebe sat down at the table and poured herself some coffee. She bit into a pastry, then put it down. Worry churned her stomach too much to eat. She wished Lewis would come and tell her what had happened.

Her wish was granted a few moments later when he entered, making her heart leap. He sent Molly away and took the chair beside her. "Michael was unable to enlighten me." His mouth turned grim. "But he is looking into it."

His brown eyes usually so vibrantly warm looked shuttered. She longed to hear what took place between him and his brother-in-law, and the questions hovered on her tongue. She poured a cup of coffee, added cream, and set it before him on the table.

Lewis nodded his thanks and stirred in a chip of sugar. "Laura's brother has promised to find out what he can."

How dreadfully defeated and tired he looked. He declined the plate of pastries she'd held out to him and drank deeply from his cup. She wondered if he dreaded that the truth might stir up further concerns for him. What happened to Laura before and after she left his house, had caused him great distress. And it wasn't at an end. She edged forward on her seat and leaned over to touch his hand. "I am sorry you have to go through this, Lewis."

He caught her hand and kissed it. "I appreciate that, Hebe." He smiled. "You have infinite patience, which I don't deserve."

"I want to help if I can," she murmured longing to reach out and stroke his dark head. But how could she? She'd never felt so inadequate. If only they could make love, but that seemed more unlikely than ever.

"You are helping, Hebe," he said softly. "Just by being here." He finished his coffee and stood. "As I've promised Michael I won't give the letter to Bow Street yet, there is nothing we can do but wait. So there's no reason not to make a start on the statue, as planned."

Hebe returned her cup to the saucer. Her confidence seemed to have plummeted to her slippers. "I have an appointment at a modiste's with your sister at three o'clock."

"We shall stop work before then." He walked to the door. "I'll have a tray sent up and meet you in the studio within the hour. I'm eager to begin."

The door closed behind him and his footsteps faded away. Hebe jumped up fighting her anguish. She had to face it at some point, but she'd hoped they would be on more intimate terms before she posed nude for him. Her hand shook when she pulled the cord for Molly.

An hour later, Lewis looked up when she entered the studio. "I trust it's warm enough. I've lit the fire. Let's hope the fine weather continues for the rest of the week. We can ride in the park. You'll have to be measured for a side-saddle. Make sure the modiste puts the habit at the top of the list."

He was determined to make their lives as normal as possible. Hebe forced a smile. "It won't take me a minute to change." She darted behind the screen and stood with her hands on her hot face. In fact, she was hot all over. Determined to be the perfect model whatever doubts flooded her mind, she began to undress.

Lewis had been puzzling over the letter before Hebe came in. Would he ever learn the truth of what had happened to Laura? Who was W? Did Michael know something that he wasn't prepared to tell him? He'd racked his brains for the few hours of the night left until he rose from his bed earlier. Laura had never mentioned anyone whose given name, surname or title began with W. But they were not often in one another's company. She sometimes attended engagements alone, and her days were filled with card parties, luncheons, trips to her dressmaker, her milliner, and shopping. And after they became estranged, well...

He was preparing his tools when Hebe emerged from behind the screen. "Let's begin," he said. One glance told him how uncomfortable she was. "You can be seated. Wrap the cloth about your hips, Hebe."

He raised his head from the sculpture as she slipped off the wrap. His breath left his lungs. She was impossibly beautiful, all pale creamy skin and pink-tipped nipples, a golden down at the base of her stomach. But it wasn't just her beauty which struck him as she arranged the white sheet, full breasts bouncing. There was a fresh wholesomeness about her, a virtuousness that had nothing to do with being untouched.

Lewis caught the tender concern in her eyes when she looked at him. He stood holding the chisel as if struck by Zeus' thunderbolt. Every bit as lovely as Aphrodite, Hebe was a gift from the gods. In that moment he considered himself to be the luckiest man on earth. And he must be so careful with this gift he'd been given. To protect this lovely young woman who was now his wife. He lost his desire to sculpt her, he wanted to lose himself in her arms. To make her his own.

Suddenly aware that she'd asked him a question and that he was staring, he tossed down the chisel and came around the statue to where she sat. "Sorry, what was that?"

"Is this the way you want me?" she asked, and her lush bottom lip trembled. Her eyes as blue as the Aegean implored him.

"Like this, Hebe." He grabbed the sheet while attempting to sound like the professional he'd always prided himself in being. Then he released the cloth and gazed down at her. This uncomfortable tension between them must end. He couldn't bear it a moment longer. He swallowed the lump in his throat. "Hebe," he murmured. "You are so beautiful. I can't think. I've lost my breath. What a fool I've been. I adore you."

"*Lewis.*" Hebe left the chaise longue and reached up to place her arms around his neck. The sheet fell to the floor as he pulled her close and kissed her.

He deepened the kiss as her soft breasts pressed against his chest. He drew in her flowery scent and the smell of warm woman as he moved his hands over her soft skin and her breasts, tracing the delicate bones of her shoulder blades, the curve of her waist and the swell of her hips.

Hebe explored him, running her hands over the bunching muscles in his back then sweeping down to his buttocks. Raw need and a demanding erection caused him to break away with a gasp. "I want you, Hebe. I think I always have. I need you."

"Oh Lewis! I've longed for you to need me as I do you. Desperately!"

"What a foolish fellow am I." He eased her gently down on the chaise longue and stepped away. His gaze rested on her as he tugged fiercely at his cravat and shed his coat. She lay back and watched him. She was Aphrodite, with a welcoming smile which had no place on a virgin's lips.

Naked, he came to join her, gathering her up in his arms, relishing the erotic sensation of her body against his. He pressed his mouth to hers, then traced the seam of her lips with his tongue. Her fingers tightened in his hair and she opened her mouth to him. With a rush of yearning, he deepened the kiss, his hands on her perfect bottom pulling her against his erection.

Lewis bent to kiss her firm nipples while Hebe murmured. He drew his hand up from her knee to the moist soft curls at the apex of her thighs, and teased, tantalized, and aroused her with the lightest of caresses. Hebe gripped his shoulders and her eyes became dark and unfocused. He pushed a finger gently inside her, pressing the warm fragrant flesh. She moaned and shuddered and thrashed as the sensations carried her away.

With a whimper and a gasp, she opened her eyes.

Lewis's gaze locked with hers. "I'll try not to hurt you."

Wordless, she shook her head.

He eased her legs apart and settled between them.

Hebe stilled as his heavy blunt erection pushed inside her. She was barely aware that the moan came from her at the jolt of pleasure, pain, and heat. Her hands roamed the smooth skin of his back as ripples of intense feeling washed through her. She ran her tongue over her lips, every nerve ending alive. Nothing she had ever imagined came close to this. To be one with the man she loved. Knowing she could move him to such passion gave her immense feminine power she'd never known she had. She breathed in the clean smell of him, a beguiling hint of masculine aromas and citrus shaving soap.

With a moan, Lewis's thrusts increased. Hebe's thoughts scattered, she dug her fingers into his shoulders, enraptured by the relentless, seductive, ecstasy of having him inside her.

With one hard thrust, a loud moan, and a gush of warmth deep inside, he quieted. For a moment, he lay breathing heavily, then rolled to the side, his leg still resting over her. "Did I hurt you?"

She was panting too, loose, and floaty. She reached up with a smile to trace a finger over his chin. "A little, but you made me forget it."

"This is not the best place for lovemaking." he said. "I never realized how uncomfortable this couch is. There's a button sticking into my side." He grinned. "Poor Hebe."

He climbed to his feet and offered her his hand, and when she stood he pulled her up into his arms and off her feet. He swung her around and murmured against her hair. "*Sweetheart.*" He set her down. "I long to do it again soon. But next time in our bed."

A pleasant lassitude still filled her limbs. A smile trembled on her lips at the slumberous expression in his eyes, and filled with emotion, she brushed back his hair with a hand. "I want that too. I love you, Lewis."

How could she love such a ruin of a man? he thought. "I struggle to put into words how much I've regretted tainting you with my sordid history, Hebe, but I hope soon to consign it to the past. We will have a wonderful life together."

The pain which had been buried in the recesses of his heart seemed to have eased. The wall he'd kept between them had collapsed when the reason for holding off from intimacy became clear to him. Since Laura, he'd never considered himself worthy of a woman's love. He cautioned himself. There was still so much uncertainty, the search for Marigold's and Laura's murderers, the rumors and the *ton's* scathing criticism to deal with, but he was confident he and Hebe would face it together, and together would overcome it.

"*Hebe.*" He kissed her then buried his face in her neck. "I am forever changed because of who you are and what you've come to mean to me."

A knock on the door drew them apart and sent Hebe scuttling behind the screen and Lewis grabbing his trousers and shirt.

After the footman brought in their luncheon, set it on the table, and left, Hebe emerged shyly tying the belt of her wrap.

Lewis felt alive. He gazed at the statue. It would be his *piece de resistance.* "Come and eat, Hebe. I'm fired up   and   keen   to   get   to   work."

Chapter Nineteen

LEWIS WORKED FAST, the marble chips falling at his feet on the cloth stretched over the floor. When Hebe left to dress for her sojourn with Emmy, he came to say goodbye to her in the entry hall and held her by the shoulders.

"Thomas will accompany you. He's my most reliable footman. He will carry your parcels and see you safely into the carriage. If you're concerned about anything, you must tell him."

"Molly will be with me," she protested. "Your sister might suspect something."

He shook his head. "Tell her I am a hopelessly besotted husband."

She laughed. "I cannot tell her that."

"Emmy would recognize that condition immediately." He grinned. "You have only to look at Colin."

She smiled as she settled in the carriage. The fact that he compared himself to Colin would be terribly sweet but for the disturbing mystery of the letter which seemed to hang over their heads like the sword of Damocles. She turned to wave goodbye to him where he stood in the street and trembled at the memory of their lovemaking. When he looked at her now, she found passionate desire in his eyes, unlike the expression in them before, when she was sure it was only concern and a wish to aid someone he'd rescued. She was confident that in time, what he felt for her now would turn to love. Perhaps not as he had once loved Laura, but she was willing to accept that.

Later, when she and Emmy entered the modiste's rooms, Madame LaFontaine welcomed them, called for wine and sweet biscuits then launched into a discussion on what would suit a young lady of Hebe's coloring. Madame suggested Pomona green, the color of green apples. A bonnet and a redingote of the same color, lined in slate silk over a white walking dress, sounded perfectly lovely. The modiste went on to describe a dove gray spencer trimmed with rose pink satin worn over a bright gray bombazine carriage dress. She brought out a bolt of light lavender-colored figured satin for an evening dress and talked of rosettes and sleeves made of fine net.

Hebe was measured and pinned into two pretty dresses that Madame had on hand, one of primrose and green, and the other pale blue with a triple flounce around the hem. Emmy later explained they would have been for another woman's order. Hebe was turned this way and that until her head swam. She feared Emmy would become fatigued before they were done. But once Madame was satisfied she vociferously saw them off, promising to find the perfect materials for a habit and ball gown.

"I hope it wasn't too much for you," Hebe said anxiously as Thomas assisted them into the carriage.

Emmy certainly looked well enough, her cheeks pink as she laughed. "It was fun! I'd very much like to return tomorrow when you are fitted for your habit and the decision is made for the ballgown. Afterward we can shop in Bond Street for accessories."

"I'm not sure your husband will be pleased," Hebe said. "I wouldn't want him to think poorly of me for dragging you about."

Emmy laughed. "Colin fusses so. He is a lamb really. Except when he's in court." She gave a gentle shudder. "I shouldn't like to be the hapless person quaking beneath his questioning."

Obviously, Emmy adored her husband. "Lewis has returned to work on the sculpture. He has great hopes that this one will be special."

"You are posing for it?"

Hebe's face heated. "Yes. The statue is of Aphrodite."

Emmy's pretty brown eyes gleamed. "I cannot wait to see it."

When Hebe returned home, she went straight up to the studio, pulling off her gloves. Hard at work, Lewis raised his head when she came in. "Did you order all your furs and furbelows?"

"Not all." She walked across the studio to study the statue. "Oh you've done so much, Lewis. It's wonderful." Aphrodite, bare breasted, stood on a plinth with one leg slightly bent. The draped cloth cloaked her modesty, but dropped away behind to reveal the smooth curves of her derriere. It was beautiful, but Hebe couldn't relate the statue to herself. "Emmy and I are to return to Madame's tomorrow. And then we'll go to Bond Street and visit her milliner's shop and the bootmakers and then there're gloves and...." She paused. "It all sounds terribly expensive."

"No matter. Have the bills sent to me." He kissed her.

She wrapped her arms around his waist and rested her head against his chest breathing him in. "Do you want me to pose for you?"

"Ah, no." A laugh rumbled his chest. "I would find myself wanting to subject you to that uncomfortable couch again." He drew away. "We didn't get much sleep last night. Perhaps a rest before dinner?"

Gazing into his eyes, Hebe nodded as an ache formed low in her stomach. She'd been thinking of him all afternoon.

"And you can tell me about your new wardrobe," Lewis grinned, took her hand, and lead her down the stairs.

"I shouldn't wish to bore you," Hebe said. "My father's mind seemed to wander when Mama discussed fashion." She almost gasped. Here she was talking about the past without the usual unwelcome, unbearable sadness. She would write to her mother as soon as she had a free moment and tell her how happy she was. Hebe's conscience pricked her. Here she was in absolute heaven while Mama was living in that mausoleum caring for her bad-tempered grandfather. She would couch the invitation for her to come to London in more persuasive terms.

The next morning, Lewis woke next to a fragrant curvaceous body curled up beside him in his bed. Hebe still slept. Understandable, they'd made love for half the night and she had proved to be a delightful lover, mischievous, flirty, beautiful, and very good at seduction. He smiled. Her hair in a tangle, she looked delicious and much too inviting.

He sobered at the thought of visiting Michael this morning and what he might learn from him.

Hebe stirred. "Good morning, sweetheart." Lewis gathered her close. He breathed in the scent of lavender. Her warm body sent a bolt of desire through him which he was determined to ignore. "Sadly, I must rise and send for my valet."

She reached up and eased a lock of his hair back from his forehead. "You are going to see Lord Somerville?"

"After breakfast."

"What will you do if he can't help?"

He drew away before his resolve weakened and threw back the covers. "I've been thinking about that. Laura's maid left directly after she did and now resides in the country caring for her sick mother. Guilford is little more than a half-day's ride. Lilly was never questioned about Laura's death. But she might know something. Lady's maids are in a unique position, are they not? There's not much they miss."

Hebe rose and slipped into her robe. "I wish I could come with you. Emmy and I are to return to Madame LaFontaine and afterward, we will go shopping. I imagine I won't be home until late."

He kissed her. "Enjoy the day, Hebe. If I do go, I'll try to get back before nightfall. Take Thomas with you."

His former brother-in-law was sawing into a steak in the breakfast room when Lewis was announced. Lewis joined him at the table and accepted a cup of coffee.

Michael's angry gaze sliced into him. "I need more time. There's no one I can think of who had anything to do with Laura or could have written that letter. Nor signed it, W."

"Give me the names of those Laura spent time with, Michael."

Michael's gaze swung away, and he shrugged. "No idea, Lewis. She was her own person. I accompanied her to parties, balls, and the like, but then we'd part company. She was not a young woman I needed to govern."

"You mean it was her husband's responsibility."

"You could hardly be that when she no longer lived under your roof. I wasn't even aware she was seeing Geoffrey Lancaster. Laura didn't seek my advice. Merely left me a note and took off with him. I daresay she hoped to divorce you and marry him."

Lewis clamped his lips on a rebuke. "I would have agreed to it."

Michael forked a piece of meat and chewed for a moment in silence. "I doubt Lancaster would have married her." He took a sip of ale. "Laura wasn't thinking clearly, obviously."

"Why do you say that?"

"Before she left me, she seemed nervous, I put it down to how it was between us, but now I've seen the letter, it's occurred to me that she was afraid. She'd left London with Lancaster to get away from this man."

Lewis stood and rested his hands on the back of the chair. "I will find out who this man is, Michael. I'm sorry if you want to bury the whole distressing business."

Michael jumped up and thumped the table, spilling ale, his face reddened. "By God, you're wrong, Lewis. I want his name. I want to get my hands on this devil as much as you do."

Lewis suspected that Michael's vicious condemnation of him was also directed at himself, because as Laura's brother he'd been unable to protect her. "I'll keep you informed of anything I discover, no matter how insignificant. And I should like the same courtesy from you."

Michael nodded. "You have it."

Lewis returned home and sent for his curricle. Still early when he set out for Guilford, he reached the town by two o'clock, having stopped to eat and rest his horses along the way. He continued his journey to Lilly Moore's cottage on the outskirts, a small thatched dwelling surrounded by a garden with more vegetables than flowers, and a goat tethered nearby. When he pulled up the horses, Lewis saw her bent over the vegetable patch.

Lilly's eyes widened as he entered the gate and strode toward her over the path, brushing away overhanging lavender bushes. "Lord Chesterton?"

"Good day to you, Lilly. I trust I find you well?"

Her fingers fussed with the cap over her brown hair, and she brushed the front of her apron. "I am, thank you, milord."

"And your mother?"

"Not in the best of health. May I offer you a libation?"

"No, thank you. I don't like to keep the horses waiting. I need to ask you a few questions about when you were in service to my late wife." He looked at a garden seat. "May we sit?"

She swallowed, looking uneasy. "Very well, milord."

Lewis sat back and observed her. She looked thinner, her hands red and worn, and not the pretty fresh-faced young maid he remembered. He moved to put her at her ease allowing his gaze to drift away over the neat garden. "I imagine lady's maids learn a lot about their mistresses," he said conversationally. "A lady tends to confide in them." He turned slightly on the seat to look at her. "Did my wife ever confide in you, Lilly? You left my house at the same time as Laura, so I never thought to ask you."

Lilly's gaze fell to her hands clutched in her lap. "Her ladyship did sometimes, but I'm not sure what..."

"There is a chance we may now find out who killed Laura. I have come in the hope that you might be able to help me."

She frowned, threading her fingers together. "I don't know if I can."

"It was initially thought that her death was the result of a robbery. Well, there have been several theories, but recently, a letter was found among Laura's things, signed W. A vicious threatening letter, Lilly. I need to know who my wife was seeing before she left me." He sighed. "I want to put a stop to the speculation which is still rife after all this time. And now that I have remarried, Lady Chesterton deserves an end to it too."

"Oh! Congratulations, milord." Lilly smiled. "I'm that pleased to hear it."

"So." He raised his eyebrows. Would she reveal the secrets he suspected she'd promised Laura always to keep? "It would not be breaking her trust, Lilly," he said gently. "Laura would want you to tell me."

"There was a gentleman, sir. She used to laugh about him." A small smile drifted across her lips. "We both laughed, because she said she had him wrapped around her little finger. He was just a conquest. Her ladyship enjoyed how her beauty affected men."

"Who was he, Lilly? Do you know his name?"

She pinched her lips. "Not his proper name. Just something she called him. Whip."

Lewis' intake of breath drew in a lungful of earthy garden odors. "Why Whip? Did she tell you?"

Lilly flushed and dropped her gaze. "Something indecent. Sorry to tell you that, milord," she whispered.

"Did you ever see this man?"

She widened her eyes. "Never."

"Did Laura describe this fellow to you?"

"He was big and broad-shouldered, with hands like plates," she said. "A gentleman, but there was another side to him. He was dangerous." She cast him a sympathetic gaze. "Milady liked that about him. But she said no woman in her right mind would marry him. One doesn't marry a brute, Lilly, she would say with that delightful laugh she had."

Tears flooded her green eyes. "I wondered after, if I should have written to you when I heard, but as her ladyship died far away from London in the company of another gentleman, I saw no sense in it."

Nor had he thought to question her. But even if he had, he would not have asked the right questions. His chest ached as he stood and took out his wallet removing several bills. "I am grateful you've told me this, Lilly. I would be very pleased to ease your way a little if I may." He reached out, took her hand in his gloved one, and placed the bills in it.

Lilly flushed crimson. She cast a quick glance at the window where her mother's face had suddenly appeared, then folded her fingers over the money in her palm. "Thank you, milord. I hope I've been of some help. You was good to me and I wish you and her ladyship happy."

Lewis climbed into his curricle and turned the horses' heads for home. He did not have this man's name, but he still felt he'd learned something of note. A big brutish man, and he had an inkling who that might be. The wind picked up. Dark clouds on the horizon told him a storm was rolling in. He cursed, hoping the rain would hold off, anxious to return to London and Hebe.

Chapter Twenty

HEBE ARRIVED HOME at five o'clock and discovered that Lewis, as he'd mentioned he might, had gone to Guilford. While Thomas carried in her parcels, she sank onto a chair in her bedchamber and eased off her shoes, tired after a busy day.

An indigo blue wool fabric had been agreed upon for her habit to be decorated with braid and frog fastenings. Underwear and nightgowns were purchased. Afterward, she and Emmy shopped in Regent Street and the new Burlington Arcade where a multitude of shops in one place quite took Hebe's breath away.

Hours later, with the carriage filled with her purchases, they'd stopped at Gunter's for iced refreshments before returning home.

Hebe with Molly's eager assistance, opened the hatboxes and shoe boxes, and untied the brown paper parcels containing gloves, shawls, and reticules. Everything was just perfect, and Hebe couldn't wait to parade before Lewis in a new gown with the elegant wide-brimmed Italian straw hat dressed with silk flowers.

While Molly tidied them away, Hebe walked to the window and stared down at the wet street. She nibbled on a fingernail. Dusk had fallen and with it bad weather which looked as if it had set in.

An hour later, she refused dinner, for Lewis had not yet returned. Neither was he home by ten o'clock. Molly brought in a tray of soup and sandwiches which Hebe could not eat. She insisted her maid go to bed.

The weather worsened, and lightning lit up the sky outside the window. Hebe went to bed when she'd grown tired of walking backward and forward across the carpet. It was better for her to be there if Lewis should arrive and not appear to be worried. He might have had to put up at an inn. To negotiate country roads in the dark during bad weather was dangerous. She almost convinced herself he had. He was very fond of his horses.

She lay back on the pillow and closed her eyes. Despite her unease she drifted off for a minute or two. Then she woke with a gasp. Might she have heard something? She sat up in bed. Had Lewis returned? Was he in his bedchamber not wishing to awaken her?

Hebe left the bed and put on her robe and slippers. She picked up the candle and opened the sitting room door to cross to Lewis' bedchamber.

She'd taken only two steps when an arm snaked around her middle pulling her off her feet, causing the candle to fall to the carpet, the flame stuttering. Her yell was smothered by a big hand that covered her mouth. A growl near her ear. "Where is the letter?"

A gentleman's voice. He smelled of expensive cologne. Hebe's heart banged against her ribs. She shook her head.

"I am going to take away my hand." His breath was hot on her neck. "I have a knife. If you scream, I'll cut your throat. Don't think I won't."

She nodded. With a cold twist of fear, she realized this man meant every word. He uncovered her mouth, but kept his hands on her shoulders, turned away from him. "The letter."

"I don't know what you mean."

"Let's stop playing games, we shall look for it. Unless you know where it is."

Hebe gasped. "I don't. "

"Then we shall find it." He reached down and picked up the candle. "Perhaps the library or your husband's bedchamber." He gave her a push.

"Lewis doesn't have it."

"Don't lie to me." The man growled with impatience. He pushed her hard toward Lewis' bedchamber door, and she stumbled. "If we don't find it, I shall wait for him to return and remove it by force. Now you wouldn't want that, would you?"

She shook her head and made to turn. To try to reason with him.

"Don't look at me! If you do, I shall have to kill you, Lady Chesterton. I shouldn't like to do that. I'm a reasonable fellow. I don't enjoy killing women who've done nothing to hurt me."

"Then please just let me go," Hebe pleaded as she stood before Lewis' door.

"I might if you behave yourself."

He reached around her and unlatched the door. Drops of water splashed onto her face from his wet hair. She was aware of how big he was leaning over her smelling of sweat and wet wool. "Get inside."

Hebe walked into the shadowy room, relieved to find Lewis' bed had not been slept in. "The dresser," the man urged.

Hebe pulled open drawers. "It's not here," she said after a while. "I didn't think it would be. Perhaps Lewis took it with him."

He still stood behind her. "Then that will be unfortunate for him."

"We don't know who you are. Why take such a risk? Go away now and you'll be safe."

"I don't like loose ends. I tidy them away by whatever means necessary."

His words sent a chill through her. "Perhaps the library then?" she asked. It gave her time. And the night porter might discover them. He was armed. Lewis had insisted on it.

"Very well. Lead the way. And no tricks."

As they left Lewis' apartments and descended the stairs, the man behind her all the while, Hebe wondered how he'd managed to break in. The house was locked up tight at night. Unless they'd left the front door unlocked for Lewis. She wasn't sure of the way things were done. She'd never taken much notice. Doors opened like magic and she passed through them. Now she feared if a servant did come across them they would be harmed. Could she escape this man somehow? She must think.

The corridors were empty, a lamp turned low on a table, no doubt for Lewis. The library when they reached it lay in darkness. The man still carried the candle in its silver candlestick holder. He put it on the desk.

She risked a peek. He was tall, broad, and dark-haired. He had tied his cravat across the lower portion of his face. "You'll look away if you know what's good for you," he said striding over to the desk. Keeping an eye on her, he rummaged through the papers, and opened the drawers.

She lowered her head and stared at the carpet, listening for footsteps crossing the tiled floor of the entry hall. "You don't see the letter, do you?" she asked in a loud voice. "I told you, you wouldn't."

"Be quiet or I'll deal with you."

"What will you do now?" she asked. "You won't find it here. And Lewis won't return from the country tonight."

"Then I shall have to remove it from him when he does."

An icy shiver ran down her spine. This man was cornered and extremely dangerous. He had a knife, and he might also have a pistol.

"What will you do, shoot him? You'll have the whole house awake. You can't possibly get away."

He stepped behind her and his big hands framed her neck. "I have these. He firmed his grip, making it hard for her to breathe.

Hebe's knees buckled. But before she fell to the floor he had caught her around the waist. "Don't swoon on me. You're safe for now. If you behave."

She prayed Lewis wouldn't come back tonight. Could the porter have heard them?

"You'd best leave, before the porter finds you."

"That poor fellow was too slow on his feet," the man said.

She gasped. "You've hurt him?"

"I doubt he felt much." The man closed a drawer. "Nothing here. We'll go up to your husband's bedchamber and await him."

"But he won't be back until tomorrow. You can't take on the whole staff!"

"I can manage your husband and his valet," he said. "They won't be thinking too clearly when they rush to your aid."

He prodded her hard in the back. "Out."

Hebe stumbled as her mind filled with horror for the porter. She fell to her knees, hoping to at least delay the brute. But he grabbed her elbow and heaved her to her feet. "Don't try any more tricks," he snarled.

It didn't matter what she did. He was going to kill her. The thought made her strangely calm. Hebe straightened up and opened the door. She had to distract him somehow. "Did you kill Marigold?" she asked him.

"The harlot who accosted me at Holland House?"

"Why did Marigold do that?"

"Her brother had something on me. Wanted payment."

"Seth?"

"I've dealt with that problem too."

She climbed the stairs slowly her knees threatening to give way. "What did Seth have against you?"

He pushed her hard from behind. "Ask a lot of questions, don't you?"

Hebe shuddered. How long before he killed her?

When they reached the landing, he pushed her into Lewis' bedchamber. "Seth Crabbe saw me kill a prostitute who tried to rob me in a Covent Garden alley. He foolishly decided to blackmail me. Sent his sister to Holland House to get the money. Stupid fellow."

Hebe stumbled into the bedchamber as her anxious breaths drew in Lewis' fresh citrus scent. She had to keep him talking. "Why did you kill Laura?"

"She toyed with me. Treated me like muck beneath her shoes." His voice was an angry murderous growl. "That arrogant mongrel Lancaster double-crossed me. Backed out of a scheme and cost me a fortune. So, two birds with one stone."

His words robbed her of breath. She must try not to provoke him again.

It would have been the sensible thing to put up at an inn until the weather cleared. The going was frustratingly slow, and Lewis was forced to stop to rest his tired animals more than once. But he did not intend to leave Hebe alone any longer than necessary.

When he reached the stables, he saw to his horses then strode toward the house searching for signs that anyone was awake. A candle shone out from the tall staircase window. Someone climbed the stairs to the bedchambers. It could be one of the staff although why it should be at this hour eluded him.

That it might not be a servant, set his heart beating fast as he ran through the rain for the front door. The servants' door would be locked, but the porter would be in the entry hall to admit him. To his horror, he found the door unlocked and Jeb, the night porter lying prostrate, bleeding over the tiles with a broken urn beside him. He crouched to examine him. There was a gash to his head, but the fellow still breathed. He began to come around as Lewis dragged him into the salon and laid him on the sofa. "Stay here, Jeb. Don't make a sound," Lewis said, while he tied his neck cloth around the man's head. "Someone will come and see to you in a little while."

Jeb murmured something incoherent and fell back on the squabs.

Lewis ran to the library and took his pistol from the cupboard. He loaded it then headed for the stairs. The possibility that the swine might have his hands on Hebe made Lewis sick with fear. He fought to calm himself as he swiftly gained the upper landing. Which room might they have entered? His, he decided.

Lewis took a gamble and slipped through Hebe's door. Her bedchamber lay in darkness and a quick investigation told him what he feared. The bed was empty the covers swept back as if she'd just left it.

Lewis crept into the sitting room and with foreknowledge easily found his way in the dark to his chamber door. He leaned against it and listened. Horror flooded through him like icy water at Hebe's soft voice.

"It's foolish to wait here until tomorrow," she said in a calm tone. "You won't be able to remain awake. What if my husband doesn't come home until late?"

"He'll be back soon. A man doesn't leave a delectable woman like you for long."

"The storm. It may not be possible..."

"Be quiet and take down that curtain rope. Time to tie you up, my lady. And I'd best gag you before you anger me and force me to do something I'll regret."

His fingers curling hard around the pistol, Lewis seized the latch.

Chapter Twenty-One

HEBE SHOOK WITH fear as she removed the silk tasseled curtain cords from their hooks on the wall. Did he really plan to tie her up or would he use them to strangle her?

"Turn your back," he ordered and jerked her arms behind her. He was in process of tying her wrists when the door flew open.

"Osborne!"

She gasped. "Lewis! He has a knife."

Osborne spun Hebe around and pulled her in front of him, the knife at her throat.

"What the blazes!" Lewis cried. "Hebe! Has he hurt you?"

"No," she said faintly, afraid to move.

"You hurt a hair on my wife's head and you're done for, Osborne." Lewis's pistol wavered. He took a step forward.

"Careful," Osborne warned.

"I never expected it to be you," Lewis said as if trying to distract Osborne from his purpose. I suspected Nicholas Thorn."

Behind her she could feel Osborne straighten and preen. "Thorn is a gutless bully. All piss and wind."

"Why show your hand? You might have got away with it," Lewis said. "Whip! Of course. You were once Chief Whip for the Whigs were you not?"

"Laura found that amusing. I couldn't chance it. When Michael spoke of the letter, I had to have it. He was foolish to put it about in White' Club on your behalf. Are you going to shoot me, Chesterton?"

"Let Hebe go, Osborne. She has done nothing to you. We can settle this between us."

Osborne grunted. "I doubt that would serve me well. This delightful lady is my key to survival. But if you don't drop that gun I'll cut her throat."

"You hurt her, and I'll kill you," Lewis growled. He threw the pistol onto the carpet and took a step back.

"You won't get the chance," Osborne snarled his grip tightening.

Osborne's breath feathered Hebe's hair. She cried out. "Oh, God. Stop this, please!"

In the scuffle the cravat had fallen from Osborne's face. She searched his broad visage reflected in the mirror, the faint gleam of sweat over his cheekbones. He was taut as a wire and breathing fast, a cold blank look in his eyes. He was a killer, and wouldn't hesitate to kill them both. She choked out a cry as the knife dug into her neck, and grew still, a pulse throbbing at her temple.

"First, the letter if you please," Osborne said.

Lewis put a hand to his coat.

"Slowly," Osborne said.

Lewis withdrew the letter.

"Burn it." Osborne breathed faster, the stench of his sweat sharp in her nostrils.

Lewis held the paper up to the candle. It caught, and burst into flames. He threw it into the fireplace. "Let Hebe go, now!"

Osborne backed away toward the door pulling Hebe with him.

The door suddenly opened. Dunstan, Lewis' overly zealous valet poked his head in.

"Go away, Dunstan," Lewis roared.

With only one candle in the large room half lay in shadow. Dunstan peered shortsightedly at them. He uttered a dismayed squeak. "I hadn't realized you'd returned, my lord, I'd forgotten to take your shirts to the..." He stopped, and horror crossed his plump face. "Please excuse me." He turned away.

"Come in, Dunstan," Osborne said. "And join us. I insist."

With a confused look, Dunstan opened the door wider. His gaze on Osborne, he stumbled as he entered.

Distracted by the valet, Osborne allowed the knife to slip slightly from Hebe's throat. She pushed away, falling to her knees.

"No you don't," Osborne snarled bending down to her.

Lewis scooped up the gun.

An explosion, and the rank smell of gunpowder filled the room.

Two bodies fell to the floor.

Lewis rushed to Hebe's side. He helped her to her feet. "Is he dead?" she asked in a whisper.

"I think so." Lewis glanced at Osborne's prostrate body. The ball had found his heart. He turned to

Dunstan who had fainted and was now weakly pulling himself into a sitting position on the floor. "All right there, Dunstan?"

"I doubt I ever shall be again, milord." Dunstan dusted his trousers with a grimace. "I'm profoundly glad you dealt with that nasty fellow, whoever he was."

"Pour yourself a brandy, and one for my wife, if you will." Lewis strode to the bell pull. "We must send for the Bow Street magistrate."

Within an hour, Hebe was dressed and sitting in the salon drinking coffee. Half the staff were awake, and the reception rooms were bright with candlelight.

When the magistrate arrived, Lewis pulled the letter from his pocket as he explained how Osborne's death came about.

When Hebe gasped, he explained to her that he'd burnt the map he'd drawn to guide him to Lilly's house in Guilford.

During the following two hours, the body was removed to the morgue, and a doctor arrived to treat the night porter. He attended to the cut on Hebe's neck where the knife had pieced the skin.

Finally, the house fell silent, and retiring upstairs, Lewis joined Hebe in bed.

Hebe lay with an arm over his chest. "It was all so horrible. Are you all right, darling?" she anxiously asked.

"I'm just thankful he didn't hurt you."

Hebe shuddered. "He had such a refined voice. If I'd met him in a ballroom, I would never have guessed at his violent nature."

"Laura came to realize it. And feared him."

"Yes, she would have." She shuddered. "He had the coldest eyes."

"She should've come to me," Lewis said trying to hide his anguish. "Asked for my help."

"She would have been ashamed as well as frightened," Hebe mused, "because her behavior would rebound on you and her brother." She stroked his hair back from his forehead and kissed him. "Her association with Lord Lancaster was to keep her safe, put an end to her fears. But you can never be sure, Lewis. You must let it go."

He sighed. "First thing in the morning I'll send a note to Michael."

"He will be pleased."

"Relieved to put this behind him, certainly."

"And the *ton* will hear of it and know you are innocent," she said, with an encouraging smile.

"The newspapers will get hold of it. A lord of the realm committing murder is big news." Lewis sighed and smoothed his hand over the curve of her hip. "Osborne might have gotten away with it. Hard to bring a lord to justice."

"He took a big chance coming here. He must have feared you'd found out about him."

"It looks that way. Once having learned about the letter from Michael, Osborne came with the intention of killing me and whoever got in his way." His hand firmed at her waist. "He was a man who fed off violence. He'd avoided capture before so must have been convinced he would do so again."

"Oh, Lewis!" She buried her face in his neck.

"We'll go to the country next week, sweetheart. For a month or so. We'll ride and enjoy the peace and quiet. And I've promised Dunstan some country air to settle his nerves."

"What about the statue?"

"I'll finish it first. Not much to do now."

"Will you sell it?"

"Never." Her body still trembled.

Lewis drew her to him. "Dear God, Hebe, if I'd lost you... I love you so very much."

"Oh Lewis. I love you too!"

She was here, and she was his. His anchor, his searing passion, his peace. He lifted her chin and pressed   his   mouth   to   hers.

Chapter Twenty-Two

LEWIS HAD BEEN toiling hard for a week. He tossed down the file. "One needs to know when to stop. Any more and I'll ruin it."

Hebe replaced her teacup in its saucer and left the table to inspect the marble Aphrodite. Sensuous and elegant, her bare feet resting on a plinth, she gleamed in the sunlight, so smooth that Hebe was drawn to stroke a hand over the statue's shoulder. "She is very beautiful, Lewis."

He placed an arm around Hebe's waist and smiled at her. "I had a beautiful model."

"Where will she be displayed?"

"In one of the niches on the staircase. I plan to replace a statue there."

He meant the bust of Laura. For a moment, Hebe wanted to protest. Whatever his first wife had done, Laura did not deserve her horrible death. Hebe felt strongly that the evidence that she'd lived and had been undeniably lovely should not be hidden away. She pulled back to search his serious brown eyes. What Laura had done and how she'd died still hurt him. Perhaps it always would. "What will you do with that one?"

"Give it to a gallery."

She nodded, pleased. "The bust is exquisite. It deserves to be viewed."

He kissed her cheek. "You're a remarkable woman, Lady Chesterton."

She sighed as she studied the statue. "No. A mere mortal, I'm afraid."

"A flesh and blood goddess," Lewis said. "And what a lucky fellow am I?"

She shook her head with a laugh. "I must leave you, I'm afraid. I have to advise Molly about what to pack. This afternoon I plan to visit Emmy. Confined to the house, she complains of being most dreadfully bored. I shall describe my new gowns, and Madame's inspiration for my ballgown. That is sure to entertain her for a little while. But I fear I will then have to read the newssheets with her and discuss the latest gossip."

Lewis pressed a kiss to her lips. "Take Thomas."

She raised a finger to stroke along his jaw. "We have nothing to fear now."

His gaze firmed. "Nevertheless."

"You are turning into Colin," she accused.

Lewis looked rueful. "I am now in sympathy with him."

Hebe shook her head and pretended to be exasperated. It really pleased her that he cared so much. She left him and walked down to her bedchamber. It was difficult to grasp the fact that the frightening mystery no longer hung over them. The Bow Street Runner, Mr. Bright, had called to tell them that Seth Crabbe's body had been found in an alley in the Seven Dials. He'd been stabbed and had been dead for some time.

As expected, the newspapers were filled with the details of Lord Osborne's murderous dealings, and friends informed them the subject was on everyone's lips. Laura's brother had even stood up in the House and apologized to Lewis. It all served to calm the waters, but Hebe still feared the *ton* would not accept her. And after all Lewis had been through, she would hate to have that happen. Lewis believed a couple of months away from London would banish the gossips, but Hebe was not so sure.

As the coach traveled along the country lanes sprinkled with daisies and blackthorn blossom, Lewis held Hebe's hand in his, surprised at how much he looked forward to showing her his country home. "Where exactly was your father's estate?" He needed to hear more about Hebe's past life, to fill in all those years when he hadn't known her.

"Charlbury. In the Evenlode valley. Our land bordered Wychwood forest."

A mere two days ride from his estate, he thought and made a silent promise to Hebe.

She was telling him about fishing in their stream as a child with her father, but stopped to crane her neck out of the window as their coach entered through the gates and traveled along the driveway to Chesterton Manor.

"I can see the roof and chimneys above the trees." She turned back to him, blue eyes dancing.

She looked so endearing that his heart hammered in his chest. He felt a burst of pride, and something close to pure joy as the Tudor mansion came into view, its warm brick walls partly obscured by creeper. Spring had wrought its magic on the garden. The huge crabapple tree was a froth of pink and white blossom and the sweet scent of honeysuckle filled the air.

"Oh, my goodness. It's charming," she murmured, as he assisted her from the carriage. She tucked a small gloved hand through his arm, her pretty smile, and the dimple at its corner, all he could see of her face beneath the brim of her bonnet. She uttered a gusty sigh. "I wish we could stay here forever."

Lewis also found the idea appealing. When Sarah answered the door, he escorted Hebe inside and introduced her to his housemaid. The peaceful atmosphere settled over him as it used to do. Determined that their weeks here would be spent in lighthearted enjoyment and the dark past banished, he led Hebe into the great hall with a massive inglenook fireplace at one end. "We'll ride into the village this afternoon. The villagers will want to meet you."

"Heavens," she murmured, her face turning pink. She removed her hat and patted her hair. Then ran a hand over the intricately carved woodwork on the staircase before going to view one of his statues which graced a corner. An oil painting hung on the oak paneled wall caught her eye. It was of Lewis as a youth, holding the reins of a chestnut stallion, his dog, Billy, at his feet.

"You look as if you want to mount the horse and ride away," she said with a laugh, "and I suspect that Billy wants to join you."

Lewis grinned. "That describes us both perfectly."

"A trifle impatient?" she asked with a mischievous smile.

He was forced to tamp down the urge to press her against the door and kiss his way from her tempting lips down to the rise of her breasts. Sarah had reappeared. She was with Mrs. Priddy, the housekeeper, and the carriage carrying his valet and other members of the staff, had just rattled its way around the corner of the house.

Lewis introduced Hebe to the housekeeper. "Some of Cook's excellent buns which rival Sally Lunn's with our tea please, Mrs. Priddy. But first, I wish to show Lady Chesterton the rest of the house." His heart warmed at the prospect of sharing his favorite place with her. But right now, he most wanted to be alone with her.

An orange cat came to greet them with a loud mew. Lewis scooped the cat into his arms. "Caught any mice, Poppy?" He grinned. "What Poppy lacks as a mouser, she makes up for in charm."

"Indeed she does." Hebe stroked Poppy's fur and was rewarded with a loud purr. "You're a fine looking cat."

After giving Hebe a glimpse of the reception rooms Lewis took her hand and led her upstairs, with the cat following.

Chapter Twenty-Three

THE DAYS PASSED in a blur, filled with delightful discoveries, about each other as well as the estate. They made love endlessly, talked late into the night and slept until almost noon. Then famished, they breakfasted, rode over the meadows, with Lewis' two greyhounds following, tongues lolling. Or they wandered the land on foot, through the apple orchard where the bees buzzed among the blossoms which reminded Hebe of Aunt Prudence, until Lewis drew her against a trunk and angled his mouth to meet hers. Then all her thoughts were of him.

They visited the neighbors, rode into the village, and stopped traffic when a crowd gathered in the street to meet her. The same occurred when they attended Sunday service at the gray stone church.

At the beginning of the third week, Lewis propped his head in his hand as he lay in bed beside her. "Shall we go to Bath for a few days?"

Hebe felt lazy, but the prospect of viewing the Cathedral, shopping on Pulteney Bridge, visiting the Pump Room and promenading the streets called to her. "Oh yes, lets."

"We could spend the night there," he said a glint of a smile in his brown eyes. "And then we might travel on to Charlbury," he said casually.

She sat up, her eyes wide. "You'd like to view my old home?"

"We could find out if your dog remembers you. Doesn't a neighbor have him?"

Hebe drew in a breath. "Rex? Oh, Lewis! I do love you!" She rolled on top of him and nuzzled his neck, enjoying his deep chuckle rumbling beneath her.

Lewis' hands slid along her spine and cupped her derriere. "The bottom that inspired a statue of Aphrodite," he murmured and pressed a kiss on her ear.

"You said it was a mosaic in..." she began but her words were swept away by his kiss.

Three letters awaited them when they returned to Chesterton Manor with Rex, a large silky-eared black dog of indeterminate species, who was nowhere near as fleet of foot as Lewis' greyhounds, although he kept trying. Lewis had delighted in Hebe and the dog's happy reunion. The neighbor, a Mr. Marksville had taken good care of the animal. But it was plain Rex considered himself to be Hebe's dog, so with good grace, the gentleman returned him to his mistress.

In the Evenlode valley, they'd stopped to view Hebe's old house from the road, a large manor house built of Bath stone with the majestic forest in the distance. Hebe sighed and sniffed into her handkerchief, but when Rex jumped onto the seat in concern, she hugged the dog and turned grateful eyes to Lewis. He smiled, delighted that she was happy. This trip had been a gamble and might have been disastrous, but it had turned out very well indeed.

Lewis sat on the bookroom sofa with Rex stretched out on the rug beside Poppy, the dog having made his peace with the cat after a cautious beginning. Lewis opened the letter from Colin, while Hebe seated beside him, read Emmy's. It appeared, from Colin's point of view, the birth had been a very worrying time. Colin had feared Emmy would not survive a long perilous labor. But he was delighted to announce a new member to the family, a daughter, Catherine Anne. Colin was perfectly comfortable with one child and had no need for an heir.

"Emmy says the birthing went as well as expected. She adores her daughter, but she plans to give Colin a son," Hebe said looking up from the letter.

Lewis chuckled. "It appears Colin might have other ideas. Although with time he may change his mind. Emmy is a healthy young woman."

"I hope to give you a son," Hebe said gazing at him fondly.

Lewis' chest tightened. He was suddenly in accord with Colin, giving birth could be dangerous. "Let's allow nature to take its course," he said, guardedly.

"I may even be pregnant now," Hebe said, a hand on her stomach.

"Do you think so?" Mixed feelings rushed through him: joy, excitement, trepidation, as he fondly regarded his wife. Hebe had blossomed since they'd come here. Her cheeks pink, her blue eyes as bright as the carpet of bluebells in the wood.

"It's too early to tell, silly," she said, affectionately stroking his hair.

"Mm. What about the other letter?"

"It's from my mother." She unfolded the paper and read.

"Well, is she coming to visit?"

"No, not yet. Mama says Grandfather still needs her."

"Your mother enjoys being needed," he said gently.

"At first I thought she was saying it to put my mind at ease. But I honestly believe Mama does like caring for Grandfather. And, surprisingly, after a bad beginning, it appears he has grown fond of her."

"Shall we hold a ball when we return to London? We'll invite your mother, your aunt, and your grandfather."

"A ball?" Hebe's heart began to beat fast. She clutched the letter in her hands. "I wonder if Aunt Prudence will come? I'm sure Grandfather won't."

"No, but your mother will, and that's all that matters."

"Yes, I hope to see Mama restored to her old life."

"And for her to see you safe and well," he said looping an arm around her shoulders.

"What if those we invite don't wish to attend?"

"They will, my love. Some out of true friendship and others from curiosity."

Hebe nodded. "That sounds very much like the *ton*."

She rested her head against his shoulder.

Epilogue

Mayfair, London, Six Weeks Later

EVERY INVITATION TO the ball had been accepted. Whether out of curiosity, or to invite them back into the fold, Hebe had no way of knowing. Lewis assured her it was the latter, but she remained jittery. She wanted this ball to be special for his sake as well as her own.

Her mother had come to London with Hebe's grandfather. They stayed at the earl's home, Longford Court. Grandfather's health had apparently improved, but Hebe doubted he would be well enough or even desire to attend the ball.

The reception room doors had been folded back to form one long room, the furniture removed. Chairs and sofas and occasional tables now lined the walls. The twin chandeliers sparkled after having been taken down and cleaned, and a three-piece orchestra set up on a dais for the dancing. Cook and the kitchen staff created an array of tasty dishes to tempt the guests, the footmen ready to serve them chilled champagne. The servants had been busy for weeks and were to be rewarded with a party of their own below stairs.

Hebe conferred with Mrs. Priddy concerning any last minute concerns. Now satisfied, she returned to her bedchamber where Molly waited to dress her in the pale blue satin ballgown. Madame LaFontaine had exceeded all Hebe's expectations. The embroidered gown had a ruched and padded hem, its tightly fitted bodice cut in a low square to show off the diamond necklace and earrings which were a present from Lewis.

At nine o'clock Hebe came down to join Lewis to greet their guests.

His eyes warmed, and he kissed her cheek. "You take my breath away."

"And you're very handsome." In his dark evening clothes Lewis was devastatingly attractive. She was glad he was hers and no ambitious marriage-minded mamas could cast a speculative eye on him.

The statue, Aphrodite, now sat in an alcove on the staircase. "What if some guests know I was the model?" she asked, horrified.

"We'll just have to cope with the envy," Lewis said with a chuckle.

Hebe blinked. "Envy?"

"Why do you think I placed it there before the ball? I'll enjoy the prospect of gentlemen envying me my gorgeous wife."

She narrowed her eyes at him and took his arm as the first guests began to arrive.

As Stubbs announced them, a maid took their cloaks and wraps, and a footman directed them to the ballroom.

When the butler opened the door again, Hebe rushed forward. "Mama!" Her mother was dressed in a beautiful dark blue silk gown, the family sapphires adorning her throat and ears.

"Hebe, how beautiful you look. And Lewis so handsome!" She kissed their cheeks then turned as Hebe's grandfather entered leaning on his cane, a hand on Aunt Prudence's arm.

"Grandfather! And Aunt Prudence!" Hebe cried, coming to kiss her aunt's cheek. "How good of you to come."

Grandfather bowed his head. "Good evening, Hebe, Chesterton."

Aunt Prudence wore a new purple gown with the feathers in her hair dyed to match. Brilliants sparkled here and there like tiny stars. "Ah, you both seem content." She nodded at Lewis. "The planetary systems never lie."

"It is good indeed to see you here and looking well, sir."

"Of course. Wouldn't miss it," Grandfather said, looking a good deal brighter than Hebe remembered.

"Is that a new gown, Mama?"

Her mother smiled. "Your grandfather has been most generous."

Hebe admitted to being surprised. "You are happy in Tunbridge Wells, Mama? You don't wish to live here with us?"

She patted Hebe's cheek. "My dear girl. I am very busy. I spend the evenings playing faro and chess with your grandfather. I'm at present rearranging the reception rooms, which have become fusty and dull. The head gardener consults with me over the planting. So you must not worry. But should you need me in the future, of course I will come immediately."

Lewis gestured to Thomas, and he hurried forward. "Escort Lord Longford and the ladies to the drawing room. Ensure they are made comfortable."

"Is that the Earl of Longford?" a lady asked as she came through the front door.

"I believe it is," her husband replied. "He hasn't been seen for so long I thought he'd passed away. Good to find him amongst Society once more."

Hebe was very grateful to her grandfather for coming. He no doubt knew his presence would dignify the occasion and aid her and her mother's return to polite Society.

As more carriages began to queue up outside in the street, Lewis tucked her hand into the crook of his arm. "Have I told you how much I adore you, Hebe?" he whispered in her ear.

"You have, my lord," she said as another couple entered.

"In case there's any misapprehension, I shall endeavor to show you later."

Her cheeks warm, Hebe stepped forward with Lewis to receive another couple. "Mr. and Mrs. Grimes. How good of you to come."

A Legend To Love Series

Chapter One Excerpt from:

The Duke of Darkness
A Legend To Love

Chapter One

North Wales
September 1819

Thump

THE DUKE OF RHUDDLAN'S hand flew to the back of his head as he pitched forward over the neck of his horse. Stars exploded before his eyes and pain spread through his skull, while sticky warmth began to ooze through his fingers. He managed to sling an arm around the horse's neck to keep himself from falling off, but only just. The sudden clinch made the poor beast panic and it started thrashing about, determined to dislodge Rhuddlan. The tighter he held on, the harder the horse bucked, until it succeeded in dumping its ducal rider onto the muddy road.

Rhuddlan landed on his side, his head bouncing mercifully off his arm—flung up at the last moment to shield his face from the impact—rather than the ground. He lay there for a moment or two with his eyes closed, trying to clear his mind and take stock of his body.

But when he opened his eyes, he saw only darkness.

He held a hand up to his face, close enough for him to smell the damp earth on his fingers, but his eyes registered nothing. Rolling onto his back, he spread his arms out wide and shut his eyes again, hoping that the next time he opened them his vision would be restored.

It wasn't.

"Your Grace!" a voice called from somewhere far away. "Your Grace, are you hurt?"

He struggled to sit up, loath to appear weak before a stranger. But a great wave of dizziness washed over him and knocked him back to the ground.

Fabric swished in his ear as if someone in a gown or long robe had knelt down beside him. A cool, calloused hand smoothed his brow, stroked his cheek. The blackness began to fade when he opened his eyes once more, but it was replaced by a world twirling like a demented ballerina and he shut them tight again.

"Your Grace, don't move for a moment. You've had a nasty fall."

The voice was feminine, English, and he heard its owner suck in a breath when her fingers met the blood oozing from his wound.

"I assure you, madam, that I—"

"I beg your pardon, Your Grace," the voice interrupted, "but if you're about to tell me you're perfectly well, then you can save your breath. I can see very well what kind of state you're in."

Her tone was brusque but polite and Rhuddlan's world was still spinning, so he held his piece. He was clearly in need of assistance, and if this girl had plans to finish him off she'd have done so by now.

"Very well," he murmured, heartened that his words were properly enunciated, not slurred and sloppy like his thoughts. "What do you suggest?"

He heard a second figure join the first, kneeling on the road beside him. "First, we stop the bleeding, Your Grace. Can you sit up if we help you?"

Another woman, older by the sound of her voice and Welsh. Rhuddlan started to nod, then thought better of it. "I believe so."

Two arms slid across his back and slowly levered him into a sitting position, holding him there as someone pressed a cloth to the base of his skull.

"How bad is it?" he asked, hoping the women didn't hear the apprehension in his voice.

They were both silent for a long moment before the younger one spoke. "It's messy."

"Head wounds do tend to bleed a lot," he returned slowly. He'd certainly seen enough of them on the battle field to know.

"Do you know what happened, Your Grace?"

He pressed his lips together. It could have been a random attack. God knew Rhuddlan tried to take care of the people who depended on him, but not everyone appreciated his methods. Yet he was nearly certain his brother Nick was behind this, quite possibly the Duke of Cumberland, too. The pair of them had been thick as thieves for the past three years, united in a single purpose: to remove Rhuddlan from power and gain control of the dukedom's finances.

But Rhuddlan said none of that aloud. "I didn't see who it was," he answered instead, which was true enough. "I didn't even see what was thrown."

"We should get you out of the road, Your Grace," the older woman said. "Do you think you can walk?"

He opened his eyes, keeping them cast downward toward the dirt. The road was still spinning, but not as fast as it had been. He cautiously lifted his lids and tried to focus on the women assisting him, but the effort—and the glaring sun—only nauseated him. "Slowly, perhaps."

They got him to his feet and helped him shuffle from the road to a nearby cottage, while a black blur that might have been a dog led the way. The distance must only have been a dozen yards or so but they seemed to take hours to cover it, and Rhuddlan was exhausted when at last they set him in a hard wooden chair. The older woman disappeared with a glance at her associate that he couldn't quite make out.

"Mrs. Davies will fetch a physician, Your Grace, and see to your horse."

Rhuddlan twisted around trying to look at the younger woman as she stood behind him, but she turned his head back and bent it slightly forward.

"You must be the healer, then," he said.

"The healer?"

He felt a cloth once again pressed against his wound and suppressed a grunt of pain. "I assume that's why you stayed with me while..."

"Mrs. Davies," she supplied.

"...while Mrs. Davies finds my physician and horse."

"Mrs. Davies is better with horses than I am. It takes no great skill to hold a cloth to a wound."

He'd been left in the care of a girl devoid of competence? He propped his elbows on his thighs and dropped his face into his hands. "Who are you, then, if not a healer?"

"Miss Stone, Your Grace. I mostly make my living with a needle and thread."

At least he'd have someone to sew up his scalp if the physician failed to appear. "You live here with Mrs. Davies?"

"I live here. She lives next door."

This stretch of land was part of the Rhuddlan estate—small farms and cottages with kitchen gardens leased to families that couldn't afford to purchase property of their own. "My tenants, then."

"Yes, Your Grace."

"Have you ever met my brother?"

"Which one?"

Rhuddlan pressed the heels of his hands into his eyes. His elder brother—the one who should have inherited the dukedom—had been killed fighting at the Battle of New Orleans four years ago. Rhuddlan didn't think of him as often as he used to, but the memories still hurt when they surfaced.

"Lord Nicholas," he answered tightly. Thoughts of his younger brother were painful, too.

"I haven't had the pleasure."

She said it with no great enthusiasm in her voice, yet no hostility either. He supposed she could have been lying, but came back to the realization that if she'd wanted him dead or incapacitated she could easily have seen to it by now.

"Perhaps you should lie down, Your Grace. My bed is just through that door—"

He wanted to protest, but between the dizziness and pain he couldn't bring himself to react with anything except relief. "Yes, thank you."

She took one of his hands and clamped it to the back of his head, holding the cloth in place, then slipped one arm around his waist and hoisted him to his feet. She was several inches shorter than he and Rhuddlan wasn't sure how she managed to keep him from crashing to the floor, but he was delivered safely to a narrow bed and sank down onto it, taking extra care to lie on his side.

The next hour was a blur of misery. His wound eventually ceased bleeding, and the cottage finally stopped spinning long enough for Rhuddlan to take in his surroundings. But the nausea refused to retreat, nor could the physician seem to banish the feeling when he arrived. The man set his case on what looked to be a crude dressing table, pushing a plain wooden hairbrush and some faded ribbons aside to make room for his phials, but the concoction he mixed up was as foul tasting as it was useless.

Rhuddlan dismissed the man, and carefully laid back down on the surprisingly soft sheets until Miss Stone roused him an indeterminate time later. By then the scent of his own blood had overpowered the smell of mint that seemed to be infused into the sheets, and he was ready to return to his own home.

"Your carriage is here, Your Grace," she said softly, laying a hand on his shoulder. "The coachman has brought a stable lad with him to see to your horse, as well."

"Good. Thank you." He allowed her to help him sit up, then to stand. "I will not forget the kindness you've shown to me today."

Her gaze drifted to the floor. "I only did what any decent person would do."

"Nevertheless," he replied, watching a few loose strands of blonde hair slide across her cheek. For a brief moment, he wondered if her hair was as soft as it looked or if his vision was still distorted. "I will remember it."

The coachman came in at that moment, and took over the support of Rhuddlan from Miss Stone, loading him into the carriage for the short drive back to Rhuddlan Hall. His head had cleared a little more by the time he arrived at the front door, and his principal secretary, Ian Vaughn, who appeared moments after the footman shut the big front door behind his master, was barely spinning at all.

"Your Grace." Vaughn dipped his head in a short bow. "Would you allow me to assist you—"

"I can walk on my own," Rhuddlan replied. His voice sounded gruff, but after nearly ten years in service to Rhuddlan, Vaughn was no doubt used to his employer's moods. "Come along, we have much to discuss."

Once the door of the study was closed, Rhuddlan made for the green velvet sofa and lowered himself upon it, motioning to Vaughn to close the heavy curtains that framed each window. He wasn't about to lie down in the presence of another person, particularly a subordinate, but the soft cushions would be more comfortable for his aching body than the stiff oak chair at his desk, and the darkness helped relieve the discomfort of the harsh sunlight.

"Where would you like to start, Your Grace?" Vaughn asked, settling himself at his own, smaller desk covered in stacks of books and papers. "With the incident this afternoon?"

"What do you know about it?"

Vaughn cleared his throat. "I spoke to Mrs. Davies when she came here. She told me that you'd been injured, but didn't know the particulars."

"A blow to the back of the head," Rhuddlan clarified.

"You think it was Lord Nicholas?"

Rhuddlan closed his eyes briefly, fighting a wave of nausea when he opened them again. "It could have been random."

Vaughn frowned, glancing at his shoes before meeting his employer's eyes again. "It could have been anyone, Your Grace. But given your brother's hostility toward you, and the encouragement he receives from the Duke of Cumberland..."

Rhuddlan sighed, more heavily than he'd intended. Nick was nearly nine years younger than he was, and had been his constant companion when they were boys despite the difference in their ages. They'd drifted apart a bit as they grew older, further still when Rhuddlan and their oldest brother purchased commissions in the Royal Army and marched away to fight in Britain's wars. When their father died and Rhuddlan inherited the dukedom, Nick had turned to Prince Ernest Augustus, the Duke of Cumberland and the King's fifth son, to fill the void.

"Cumberland, yes." The complete opposite of Rhuddlan, who no doubt promised Nick power and wealth that his own brother wouldn't give him. "Any sightings of him?"

"No, Your Grace. As far as anyone knows, he's still in Hanover."

"That's good, at least." Not that a little thing like distance would stop him—or Nick, for that matter—but it was something. "Have there been other incidents today?"

Vaughn shook his head. "Nothing since the mill fire."

Rhuddlan turned slightly sideways and rested his temple against the back of the sofa, inhaling the scent of the leather-bound books on the shelves behind him. A fire had been deliberately set three days ago in a grain mill on another part of the estate. It had happened in the middle of the night and no one had been hurt, but every person employed there was now looking for a new way to provide for their families.

"And no proof who set the fire?" He knew very well there wasn't, but he couldn't help asking.

"No, Your Grace," Vaughn repeated. "Though the food baskets were delivered today. The next set will be delivered a week hence."

That made Rhuddlan's mind a little more easy. At least his people would eat. "Good. I have another task to add to your list—find out everything you can about a woman named Stone who lives in one of the thatched cottages near the road to the village. And discover what you can about Mrs. Davies, as well. She is Miss Stone's next door neighbor."

Vaughn scribbled across a piece of paper on his desk. "Do you think they had anything to do with your attack?"

Did he? Rhuddlan shook his head, then winced as the pain overtook him. "No," he answered, closing his eyes tightly. "I doubt they would have helped me if they were the ones who caused me harm in the first place." It was more likely that at least one of them would come begging a favor of him, and he wanted to be prepared. "But I need to be sure."

"I will see to it, Your Grace."

"Good." Another weight lifted, at least for the time being. "What else have I missed today?"

"What a mess he made of your sheets," Mrs. Davies lamented, running a hand over a section of embroidery that hadn't been bloodied.

Olivia Stone suppressed a sigh. She'd worked for weeks on the pillowcases alone, pillowcases that were now covered in patchy stains from the Duke of Rhuddlan's head wound. "They may yet come clean," she replied, though even she could hear the lack of conviction in her voice.

"Certainly, and I may yet become a duchess," Mrs. Davies said with a wink. Then she sobered, asking quietly, "Do you have another set, my dear?"

Olivia pictured the soft linen she'd purchased last week, already sewn into sheets and decorated with carefully stitched honeysuckle vining along some of the edges. She'd saved for months to buy that material, planning to make the sheets a Christmas gift for neighbors.

And they were the only other sheets she possessed.

But Olivia didn't want Mrs. D. to worry—she did enough of that on Olivia's behalf as it was. "I do, yes."

"Good. You'll be over for supper tonight, won't you?"

Another reason for the Christmas gift: if not for Mrs. D. issuing her almost nightly invitation to dine with her and her live-in companion, Miss Hatch, Olivia would likely go to bed hungry more often than not. She earned money each month taking in sewing to provide for herself and her big black dog—curled up contentedly by the front door—but too many of her customers had begun patronizing the new dressmaker's shop in the village, and her income had steadily been declining. The generosity of her neighbors lessened the strain on her tight budget, and giving them good quality linen with Olivia's own embroidery was a way of saying thank you.

"I will, just as soon as I get these stains soaking in some cold water."

She bid Mrs. D. farewell and grabbed two buckets, heading toward the small stream that flowed a quarter mile behind her cottage. The water in it was always cold as melted snow, and it might be enough to get the blood out of her sheets.

Olivia was halfway home again with her buckets filled nearly to the brim when a shadow fell across her path. She sucked in a breath and held it, recognizing the smell of his expensive cologne before her eyes reached his face.

Sir George Grayson. He claimed to have been courting her for the past several months, except his addresses were anything but courtly...and even less welcome. He treated her more like prey than a potential wife, despite his professed love for her. Olivia knew it was her connections he loved, though, not her. If not for her relation to Viscount Teverton—never mind how distant it was—Sir George wouldn't have given her a second thought.

Too bad he also knew her real identity, and wasn't above blackmailing her with it.

"Aren't you going to greet me?" He came to a halt directly in front of her, a box held in one hand while the other reached for her.

She set down one of the heavy buckets and offered him her hand, trying, as usual, to disguise her reluctance. If he detected anything but willing obedience in her voice or manner, there was no telling what he'd do. "Good afternoon, Sir George."

He took her hand, giving it a hard squeeze. "Good afternoon to you, Olivia. What's the water for?"

She couldn't let him know that there had been another man in her home, but if he caught her lying to him... She shuddered internally and pushed the thought away. "Some of my linens were stained, and I need to soak them before the stain sets."

He yanked her closer to him, sloshing water onto her shoes from the bucket she still held. "Linen? As in bed sheets?"

She swallowed hard and dropped her gaze, her whole body tensing. "Yes. But it's not what you think."

"It's not what I think? What do you know about what I think?"

It was a trick question, of course. It always was. "I didn't mean to presume, Sir George."

His grip on her hand relaxed a little. He liked her best when he thought she was meek and biddable. "I'm sure you didn't. Tell me, then—what happened to your sheets?"

Olivia slid her hand gently from his, slowly setting down the other bucket of water in case she needed to run. He'd never seriously harmed her—he seemed to enjoy her fear more than her pain—but he'd threatened to do so more times than she cared to recall.

"Th-there's blood on them," she replied quietly, clasping her hands together at her waist. Perhaps this time she could quell the shaking before he noticed it.

"Blood on your sheets?" His tone was even, almost conversational. But his eyes had narrowed and his cheeks had flushed. "Who were you tupping, you little whore?"

"No, Sir George, that isn't what ha—"

"And now you lie to me about it?" He took a step closer to her, grabbing the neckline of her dress in one big fist. "What have I told you about lying to me?"

Olivia fought to control her breathing. The more panic she displayed, the longer he would torture her. "That there would be consequences," she said as steadily as she could. Part of her badly wanted to explain the situation, to exonerate herself of the wrongdoing he was imagining. But she knew that would only anger him more, so she clamped her mouth shut.

"That's right. Would you like to tell me the truth now, or do you want to find out what those consequences are?"

His words were harsh, almost a whisper, but they frightened her more than if he'd been shouting. "I am telling you the truth," she managed, fighting tears. She'd only cried in front of him once and he'd stomped away in disgust, but she couldn't be sure he'd react that way a second time. What if her tears enraged him even more?

"Perhaps I should burn down your little house, hm? With no place to live, you'd have to marry me...or freeze to death this winter." She clenched her teeth together hard to keep from responding, but he smiled. "While I'm at it, I'll put your neighbors' hovel to the torch, too. That would teach you not to lie to me, wouldn't it?"

Faint but persistent barking filtered through the air, simultaneously filling her with hope and dread, her heart racing as the sound grew louder. What would George do to the animal who came upon them? To a person accompanying the animal?

His eyes stayed focused on hers for a moment that felt like years. Then he slowly released her gown and opened the box he'd been carrying. Her eyes widened as he drew out an ivory-handled pistol and touched the tip of the barrel to her chest.

"Don't make a sound."

She nodded slowly, barely breathing as he turned and fired in the direction of the barking. Peering around his shoulder, Olivia could see her dog, Artie, loping down the hill toward them. He started when the gun fired and she pressed her hands to her mouth to stifle the scream that tore from her throat.

Artie laid his ears back and snarled, racing toward Sir George and the sound of the shot. Sir George pulled a second pistol from the box and took aim, sending the tears pouring down Olivia's face.

She gathered every ounce of courage she had and shouted, "*Loup! Arrête-toi!*" He didn't always listen when he thought she was in danger, but he'd been a herding dog before the late Mr. Davies had brought him home from Waterloo and still reflexively responded to commands given in French. Thankfully, he stopped in his tracks and dropped into a low crouch. Mrs. Davies' form crested the hill a second later and Sir George lowered his weapon, concealing it behind his back, as the smell of gunpowder hung thick in the air.

"Olivia? Are you down there?" Mrs. D. called. "I forgot to ask you—"

"I'll be right there," she called in a shaky voice, defying Sir George's order for silence once again, hoping he'd leave Mrs. D. alone if she stayed far enough away. To him, she murmured, "If I don't go up there, she'll come down here."

Sir George gave her one final glare, then jerked his chin in Mrs. D.'s direction. Olivia lifted her buckets of water and tried to walk normally, whistling to Artie to follow her up the hill. Mrs. D. held out an arm and Olivia passed her one of the buckets, threading her free arm through Mrs. D.'s, hoping to draw strength from the older woman.

"Just a few more minutes and you'll be safe," Mrs. D. whispered.

Olivia spent her remaining energy maintaining a calm countenance and a regular stride all the way back to Mrs. D.'s cottage. Once she rounded the corner into the little kitchen garden, she let go. Dropping her bucket and leaning against the stone wall of the house, Olivia covered her face and cried out her terror, her anger, her relief that no one had been hurt today. Mrs. D. hugged her, let Olivia cry on her shoulder as Artie leaned against her legs.

"How bad was it this time?" Mrs. D. asked when Olivia had cried herself out.

"You heard the shot?" It was all Olivia could bring herself to say, but it was enough to convey the danger they'd been in. Sir George had described his pistols in detail over the last few weeks, including the animals he'd killed with them.

Mrs. D. hugged Olivia to her again. "You poor girl."

"I can't live like this anymore," Olivia choked out. "What am I going to do?"

Mrs. D. rubbed Olivia's back in slow circles, and Olivia let the motion and the gentle breeze calm her, let them carry away thoughts of what could have happened at the base of the hill. When she'd cried her last, she lifted her face and wiped her eyes, bending down to give Artie his own hug and kiss. "You're a good boy, Loup Garou."

"You do have one option."

Olivia straightened, keeping one hand on Artie's furry head as she faced Mrs. D. "Teverton?"

Mrs. D. didn't react to the name, but she didn't have to. It was a discussion they'd had before. Lord Teverton was Olivia's closest living relative and head of her family, but the only thing she knew about him was that he owned an estate near Liverpool.

"What if he turns me away?"

No one could legally force Olivia to marry Sir George, but if she went to Teverton for help and he refused, her only choice would be between Sir George and slow starvation as the demand for her work continued to decline and her past slowly caught up with her.

"But what if he doesn't?"

Olivia pressed the heels of her hands to her eyes. What if Teverton was an honorable man who promised to protect her? Did she even have paper to write him a letter and ask?

"What about His Grace?" she said suddenly, dropping her hands to her sides. The breeze picked up, carrying with it the scent of the mint growing a few feet away.

Mrs. D. took a step back. "What about him?"

"Well...he's here. Teverton is all the way in Liverpool. Or at a different estate completely. And the duke ought to be amenable to my situation—if I am hale and hearty, I can continue paying my rent every quarter."

Mrs. D. shook her head faintly. "You can't mean to ask him for help."

"At least I've made his acquaintance," Olivia replied slowly. "Better the devil you know."

"Devil is right," Mrs. D. said, her mouth pulling into a pucker as if she'd eaten something sour. "I know we helped him this afternoon, but that was basic decency. You know what they say about the man."

Olivia did know. She'd borrowed a battered copy of a story called *The Vampyre* from a friend in the village the previous week, and had read it aloud to Mrs. D. and Miss H. after dinner one evening. The two older ladies had exchanged a knowing look, and it had taken some doing to get Miss Hatch to elaborate.

"The Duke of Rhuddlan," she'd said with a shudder. "Some think he's like that. A vampire."

She'd refused to speak of it further, and Olivia had let it drop. But she'd made an inquiry or two when she returned the book a few days later, and Miss Hatch wasn't the only person who thought there was something unholy about His Grace.

Olivia frowned at Mrs. D., recalling the fraught conversation they'd had about Olivia's past when Sir George had first come calling. "Does that mean you believe the rumors about me?"

Her neighbor made a little gasping noise. "Of course not! I would never—"

"Then perhaps the rumors about him are equally as malicious."

Mrs. D. stood staring for several moments, but eventually nodded. "Perhaps."

Olivia felt Artie's fur slide through her fingers as he bolted away after a rabbit. "Then I'll make an appointment to see His Grace."

She felt calm for the first time in months, despite Mrs. D.'s disapproval. Nothing in her life had immediately changed, but at least she had a feasible plan. If the Duke of Rhuddlan tossed her out on her ear she'd be right back where she started, but she tamped that fear down. One thing at a time. And now she had something she could *do*.

*** End of excerpt *The Duke of Darkness* (A Legend to Love) ***

About the Author

Maggi Andersen lives with her husband, a retired lawyer, in a quaint old town in the Southern Highlands of New South Wales, Australia. She has a BA in English and an MA in Creative Writing.

When not creating stories, Maggi reads, enjoys her garden, long walks around a town known for its beauty in spring and autumn, and feeding the local wildlife. Her kookaburras (Australian Kingfishers) prefer to be hand fed.

Maggi is an Amazon to Historical Romance author. She has published more than 30 novels and novellas many of which are bestsellers, and some nominated for awards. She writes in several genres: contemporary and historical romance, romantic suspense, mysteries, and young adult novels.

Please consider leaving a review for this book. Every review is appreciated!

Like to learn about her new releases and freebies? Join Maggi's newsletter at: **http://eepurl.com/cEqK9b**

Website: http://www.maggiandersenauthor.com
Blog: **http://www.maggiandersen.blogspot.com**
Amazon Author Page:
https://www.amazon.com/Maggi-Andersen/e/B003MJXQVG

Facebook:
**https://www.facebook.com/maggiandersenaut
hor/**
Twitter: **https://twitter.com/maggiandersen**
Goodreads:
**https://www.goodreads.com/author/show/278
6221.Maggi_Andersen**
Pinterest:
http://www.pinterest.com/maggiandersen.com

Follow Maggi on BookBub:
https://www.bookbub.com/authors/maggi-andersen
BookBub have a new release alert. They will send an
email advising of you of my latest book.

Other Books By Maggi Andersen

The Baxendale Sisters Series
Lady Honor's Debt
Lady Faith Takes a Leap
Lady Hope and the Duke of Darkness
The Seduction of Lady Charity
The Scandalous Lady Mercy

The Dangerous Lords Series
The Baron's Betrothal
Seducing an Earl
The Viscount's Widowed Lady

The Kinsey Family
Unmasking Lady Helen

Regency Sons
Captain Jack Ryder – The Duke's Bastard

Standalone Stories
The Marquess Meets His Match
The Baron's Wife
Hostage to Love
How to Tame a Rake

An Improper Earl
Caroline and the Captain
The Earl and the Highwayman's Daughter
Stirring Passions
At the Earl's Convenience
Lord Bartholomew's Christmas Bride
The Duke's Mysterious Lady
Diary of a Painted Lady

Contemporary Romantic Suspense
Waving at the Moon
Murder in Devon
With Murderous Intent
Twined
Finding Daniel

A Night of Angels: A Magical Holiday Collection
A holiday collection from Dragonblade Publishing authors.
Eleanor Fitzherbert's Christmas Miracle by Maggi Andersen
Childless widow, Eleanor Fitzherbert has resigned herself to a life alone, because most unmarried gentlemen wish for an heir. But after a young sweep gets stuck in the Duke of Broadstairs' chimney, and a handsome viscount comes to his rescue, surprising things begin to happen.

www.ingramcontent.com/pod-product-compliance
Lightning Source LLC
Chambersburg PA
CBHW061612170626
46811CB00001B/399